The Good Teacher

T0194230

The Good Teacher

a novel by
Jack Slutzky

iUniverse, Inc.
Bloomington

The Good Teacher

iUniverse books may be ordered through booksellers or by contacting:

iUniverse
1663 Liberty Drive
Bloomington, IN 47403
www.iuniverse.com
1-800-Authors (1-800-288-4677)

Because of the dynamic nature of the Internet, any web addresses or links contained in this book may have changed since publication and may no longer be valid. This is a work of fiction. All of the characters, names, incidents, organizations, and dialogue in this novel are either the products of the author's imagination or are used fictitiously.

ISBN: 978-1-4502-9171-2 (pbk)
ISBN: 978-1-4502-9170-5 (hbk)
ISBN: 978-1-4502-9449-2 (ebk)

Library of Congress Control Number: 2011901161

Printed in the United States of America
iUniverse rev. date: 4/6/11

The real heroes of the world
Are the men and women
Who take the time and
Make the effort
To make a difference
In the life of a person…
Here are just a few of their stories

ACKNOWLEDGEMENTS

My warm thanks go to Chuck Casey, Michael Colucci, Helena Coleman, Fran Filipitich, Robert Fussell, Gil Goodman, Carolyn Hamil, and Butch Mothersell.
Their willingness to give me critical advice was invaluable.

A special thank you to my wife and best friend, Adriana ippel Slutzky.
Her clarity, caring, insight, objectivity and sense of humor
Kept me on the straight and narrow…
And still does.

"Einstein would rise after the lecture and ask whether he might put a question. He would then go to the blackboard and begin to explain in simple terms what the lecturer had been talking about. "I wasn't quite sure I understood you correctly," he would say with great gentleness, and then would make clear what the lecturer had been unable to convey."

This is what effective communication, and good teaching is all about. As Aquinas put it long ago, the poor teacher stands where he is and beckons the pupil to come to him. The good teacher goes to where the pupil is, takes him/her by the arm, and leads her/him to where he/she ought to go. The former isn't worth a nickel, and the latter can't be paid enough.

May 20, 2009

Brookside University

The Jerald Winterkorn Memorial Field House

(occasion)

The P. Miller Annual Award Ceremony for Outstanding Teaching

The facility was packed to the rafters with more than 5,000 people. A large percentage of the audience composed of parents, relatives, and friends of those students scheduled to graduate the following day. The remaining space was taken up by graduate students, seniors and juniors who had experienced and supported the four award-winning faculty. Others in attendance were members of the Board of Trustees, the administration, and faculty and staff from across the university.

Dr. Bullward, Provost and Chief academic officer of *Brookside University*, a no nonsense dark skinned, tall man with a full-head of silver gray hair, a booming voice, stylishly dressed in a dark grey sharkskin suit, arose from his seat on the platform, and slowly and methodically moved to the dais while thinking to himself about a conversation he had with himself that very morning while reading the paper. The story that grabbed his attention was about a heroic woman in Afghanistan who was raped and beaten almost to death for attempting to educate women. It made him think of his own circuitous journey, the obstacles he had faced, and the struggles he had encountered towards becoming Provost. In doing so, he could not help but think about what those four talented faculty persons he would be recognizing that afternoon had endured, and had to overcome on their journey towards today.

"Ladies and Gentlemen, honored guests, as Provost of this great university, speaking for President Ellingwood, the Board of Trustees, the faculty and staff, and student body, it is my privilege to now formally welcome you to *Brookside University* to honor an eighteen year tradition, awarding the mantel of Outstanding Teacher to four of our finest faculty persons.

Before I begin, allow me to introduce Ms Rachael Steen, this lovely lady to my right. She along with her colleague Mr. Robert Malcomb will be providing interpreting services for this program. As you are probably aware *Brookside University* is the home of the International Facility for Students who are Deaf, or as we call it, I.F.S.D. I.F.S.D. is a unique college in every sense of the word. All 2,879 students are mainstreamed, meaning those students major and study at all of the other colleges that make up this university. Interpreting services, note-taking, tutoring and a myriad of other services are provided through I.F.S.D. to insure maximum learning and entry into the world of work. We are very proud that out of fifty-five universities and colleges applying for the privilege of having the facility on their campus, the federal government awarded Brookside University the honor.

In the last twenty-five years *Brookside University* had gone from a small regional college servicing roughly 3,200 students in up-state New York, to a college with an enrollment in excess of 35,000 full-time students (including 8,000 international students), more than 18,000 part-time and continuing educational students, and 2,879 students of the International Facility for Deaf Students (I.F.D.S.).

The meteoric growth, the diversity of its student body and staff, as well as being on the cutting edge of technology prompted *Time Magazine* to highlight *Brookside,* calling it a national treasure. Since that feature ran three years before, and a similar one every year since, a large number of local, state-wide, national and international media were in attendance at all major events.

This year, this day has been awarded special coverage because the newly elected *Vice President of the United States* had agreed to be guest speaker.

This is not an occasion we take lightly. Recently named for the seventh consecutive year, as one of the top five private universities in the country, we are under the careful eye of public scrutiny. What we say and do here does not stay here, but almost instantaneously becomes news in this country and abroad.

On this day and evening, we honor our faculty. Tomorrow we will honor our graduates..."

Before he could finished the sentence, the audience arose from their seats and began to wildly cheer and applaud. The Provost wisely paused, and patiently waited for the din to die down. He then continued…

"Our graduating students will be leaving us with the highest cumulative grade-point-average (G.P.A.) ever attained by a senior class. Already more than one third of the graduating class have been offered and accepted positions in government, and the private sector, with others contemplating additional offers. This year had seen more on-campus interviews than ever before, and the feedback we have received from potential employers has been superb."

More applause.

"Since this is only our opening salvo in honoring our faculty, and graduating class, I will limit my remarks to brief introductions of the award winning faculty, and to remind you of this evening's gala dinner in which our honored faculty will speak in earnest, followed by remarks of the Vice President of the United States.

Much more applause and cheering echoed throughout the field house.

The provost, a wise and experienced speaker gave the ovation ample time to die down.

"The four faculty being honored today are:

Professor Stanley MacKeon", Professor of English Literature. Professor MacKeon has been teaching at *Brookside* for the last 22 years. Before that spent 12 years at *Yale* after completing his doctorate at *Harvard*.

Professor MacKeon not only loves English Literature, but he deeply believes English Literature is one of the few viable methodologies our society has available to it to test real-world values.

He tells any and all who would listen that the reading of books is not only a necessary activity, but the gateway towards understanding the world as it evolves.

For more than twenty years there has not been a vacant seat in any of Professor MacKeon's classes.

"Professor Stanley MacKeon is a prize, and we are honored to have him on our staff. Professor please stand and approach the podium to be recognized... Professor MacKeon."

Once again the audience broke out in applause, foot stomping and whistling. A person driving by the auditorium would think a major sporting event was taking place.

A tall, red-faced, white-haired Irishman stood up from his seat on the rostrum and awkwardly pondered his way toward the podium. His girth, a result of not enough exercise as well as an excess of Irish lager led the way.

As the rousing round of applause began diminishing, a voice could be heard from the balcony, "Way to go Prof." Laughter could be heard across the auditorium. With a big smile across his face Stan MacKeon took out his glasses from his breast pocket, adjusted them half way down on his soft pudgy nose, looked over his glasses at the audience and waved a big thank you.

"Thank you from the bottom of my heart, thank you. My own words don't come close to expressing the feelings I am feeling at this moment. But being blessed with the ability to love and recall literature-at-large, please allow me to quote some great wisdom from of all places, Yiddish proverbs.

"If we thanked God for all the good things, there wouldn't be time to weep over the bad."

"When brains are needed, brawn won't help."

"It doesn't cost anything to promise and to love."

"Pray you may never have to endure all that you can learn to bear."

and lastly… "Dividends from children is more precious than from money."

With that said, he gave the audience a big smile and turned to return to his seat. The Provost stopped him and said "Professor MacKeon, please, stand here for a moment. I have a need to have these kind people in the audience hear what many students have to say about this kindly old professor.

And I quote:

"One of the best teachers I have experienced anywhere."

"He makes the words come alive."

"I never realized the power of words, and ideas before his class."

"He always found the time to help a student in need, and never demeaned a student for not understanding, or asking a dumb question."

"In his class, *Overt Sexuality in 20th century English Literature*, students sit in front of their computers waiting eagerly for open registration to begin, then as fast as their fingers type, attempt to register for that class."

"His last class is always listed as T.B.A. (to be announced) is full in the first fifteen minutes. When you consider no one but

Professor MacKeon knows what that class will entail, you can see what a great tribute that is."

Dr. Bullward paused to give the audience a moment to digest the words he just spoke.

"Every class taught at *Brookside University* includes a student feedback form. This form is collected on the last day of class, and sent directly to the department chairperson.

The department is responsible for compiling the information, summarizing it, composing a faculty feedback sheet. This includes narrative feedback and the percentage of students who responded, and getting it into the hands of the faculty person before the start of the next semester.

The feedback I have just read to you comes from students in Professor MacKeon's classes, all three classes. Those comments and others like it make it apparent why he is a most valued faculty member. Professor Stanley MacKeon.

When the ovation died down, Professor MacKeon, a little redder, waved once again to the audience, and ambled back to his chair.

"Professor Earl Starkvisor" a man of boundless energy, a man who serves as Chairperson of the Science Department, a man who is a consultant for NASA and the AMA, a man who has the reputation of being "slightly" overbearing, and no one to mess with, yet a man students flock to, to learn from. Professor Starkvisor please stand and approach the podium to be recognized."

A man no more than five feet, two inches tall, pertly hopped up from his seat and sauntered over to the podium. Earl Starkvisor glistened from the top of his bald head to the bottom of his shiny wing-tip shoes. His gray pin-strip suit looked as if it just came from the dry cleaners. The diamond tie-pin that affixed his black-silk tie to his starched white shirt gave him the appearance of a fashion blade. As a graduate student in California the importance of "dressing for success" became clear to him, and he now epitomized the adage.

"Professor Earl Starkvisor grew up loving pure science. Researching the unknown, be it the universe, the oceans or the internal structure of living organisms. If he could develop a hypothesis, research its potential impact and find a way to interest his colleagues he was in seventh heaven. Being short, bald and stocky, his own description of himself, did in no way impact on his ability to enchant, intrigue and motivate anyone he got to listen to him. In fact one of his theories as to the reason he developed his brain power, and his communication skills was because he was short, and slightly (again in his words) different. Not having the physical stature to depend on, nor to attract with, he postulated the short person developed the skills he needed to cope with childhood, adolescence and early adulthood. By the time he is ready to compete in the marketplace, the short person is, in Dr. Starkvisor's words, "heads and tails' above his/her competition.

What makes Professor Starkvisor even more unique is the fact that after he attained his doctorate in Nuclear Biology, he later earned a second doctorate in Computer Technology.

As passionate as Professor MacKeon is about literature, Professor Starkvisor is about pure science. He is ceaseless in ardently professing his intense love of science, and gives it as probably one of the reasons he has never been married."

Many in the audience began to chuckle.

In response, Professor Starkvisor reached over to Dr. Bullock, and asked if he may have the microphone. With a big grin on his face, he announced, "Yes, alas it is true ladies and gentlemen. It is true. Not a single woman has asked, nor even expressed a modicum of interest in me as a partner. It is not because I haven't tried. I really have. So if anyone in the audience might be interested in a fascinating encounter, please see me after these proceedings are completed." With this said, and a big smile on his face, Professor Starkvisor handed the microphone back the Provost.

More than a smattering of laughter could be heard in the auditorium.

"Professor Starkvisor might not have the height of Professor MacKeon, but his stature in the fields of Aero/Astro & Aquatic Science, and Computer Engineering is legendary. William Bates Director of N.A.S.A., in a speech he gave upon the successful return of *Mission Mars* stated, "though there are many people responsible for the success of this mission, one man must be thanked individually, Earl Starkvisor. His dedication to this mission, his contributions to the latest technology and his endless availability at every phase of our mission was without a doubt in my mind one of the reasons the mission went flawlessly."

"Student feedback from Dr. Starkvisor's classes varies from...

"The man is a genius, a total genius."

"He never made me feel stupid, in fact he offered to help me after class for as long as it would take to make me understand the material. I agreed, and within no-time I understood the material.

Though I am planning on changing my major next year, I will never forget him."

"His passion became my passion… dynamite!"

"Ladies and Gentlemen, it is my pleasure to present, Professor Earl Starkvisor."

A loud round of applause filled the field house. Earl Starkvisor scanned the audience, smiled, waited a few seconds, and then spoke.

"Working as a consultant in government, as well as the private sectors, I am many times asked to describe the differences between teaching at the university and other environments To do so, I tell the following story.

"A short while ago a meeting was called between the *College of Human Interactivity* (which at one time was known as the *College of Liberal Arts*), and the *College of Nano-Technology, Robotics and Computer Based Studies* (which at one time was known simply as the College of Science) to look for common ground between disciplines in order to improve productivity, and foster collegiality.

Allowing the necessary time for people to get comfortable, the chairperson began to call the meeting to order when suddenly a loud noise rang out from somewhere, and out of nowhere a genie suddenly appeared. Looking right into the eyes of the chairperson the genie said in a booming voice, "Because you volunteered to assume the awesome responsibility to chair this meeting, a task no one wanted, I will grant you and only you, whichever one of these three wishes you choose: **wisdom, beauty** or **three million dollars.**

As a person would expect from a true academic, without a moment's hesitation, the chairperson chose **wisdom**. As he verbalized his choice, a resounding boom encompassed the room, while a flash of lightening sparked and glowed with an awesome brilliance. The chairperson unable to move, sat transfixed, simply starring down at the table. Within seconds one of his colleagues nudged him and asked him to say something. Looking forlorn, then scanning the room, then lastly looking at his colleagues he said, I should have taken he money."

At first the audience was silent. Then little-by-little laughter could be heard. At that moment Dr. Starkvisor winked, shrugged his shoulders and in a pleading voice said to the audience, "come on folks, think about it."

Within seconds the audience, as a unit began to laugh. With a smile on his face that could light up the planet he said, "This ladies and gentlemen is a small taste of what my students experience."

With the calm and confidence of a man born to this life he bowed slightly, smiled broadly and sauntered back to his seat.

"Professor Nan Alderage-Gates," would you please approach the podium to be recognized.

A slim attractive woman, five feet, eight inches tall, wearing a dark brown man-tailored suit, a beige blouse with an open v-neck collar, sporting two inch heels the same color of her suit, sans jewelry rose out of her seat and confidently walked up to the podium.

Provost Bullward watching her approach the podium gave her a smile of admiration, which she gracefully returned, then continued his introduction.

"In a college that counts forty-two full-time faculty, Professor Alderage-Gates is one of only four female faculty persons, attesting to her extraordinary abilities, and dogged nature. "Breaking the glass ceiling" in a traditional man's world, facing up-hill struggles at every turn in everything she has attempted to accomplish and did accomplish, she has done with dignity, perseverance and style.

"Professor Alderage-Gates is completing her eighteenth year as a faculty person at *Brookside University...* her colleagues call her remarkable, and that is what she is, remarkable! She is not only brilliant, but as I have been told, a fierce fighter for equity, fairness, and progress at faculty and college meetings, never hesitating to share her beliefs.

"I give you. Professor Nan Alderage-Gates."

Applause.

Feeling extremely uncomfortable with all the attention, she could do no more than offer a weak smile, and a slight nod.

"Professor Alderage-Gates has gained an international reputation derived from her work in Nano-technology, while serving as recording secretary of *the International Society for Digital Development*. A society which publishes the prestigious *Nanobyte*, a monthly magazine respected all over the world.

She spent one year abroad two years ago, representing the university, by presenting papers and teaching at colleges in the Netherlands, Germany, Switzerland, France, England and finally in Scotland. Since that time we get almost daily requests for her expertise from other universities and think-tanks across the world.

Professor Gates holds an earned doctorate from *Purdue University*, a Master's Degree from *Rensselaer Polytechnic Institute* and a Bachelor of Science Degree from *Iowa State Teachers College*.

Prior to becoming a member of the faculty at *Brookside University* she worked for the *Defense Department* six years as a Digital Specialist, while being a paid consultant for the *C.I.A.* And for the six years before that, she taught three years at *U.C.L.A.*, then three more years at *Washington State University.*

Students have said about her:

"She is awe-inspiring, and has no problems expressing her passion for her subject matter."

"I really enjoyed Professor Alderage-Gates' class in spite of her disciplinary approach to teaching. She was as tough as the class's technical demands were."

"She not only preaches the gospel of nano-materials and sustainable energy technologies, but she encourages us to balance our left brain activity with our right brain. I will never forget her saying, "without technology, our world would stagnate, but without the Arts the quality of our endeavors would be worthless."

"I want to thank Professor Alderage-Gates for showing me a way. Not "the" way, but one directly applicable toward life, and the pursuit of it. Thank you for your love, trust, patience, passion, and biases."

"Without further adieu, would you please welcome Professor Nan Alderage-Gates."

Again a large round of applause resounded throughout.

"Ladies and gentlemen, thank you for your kindness. This day, and your acknowledgement will stay with me for the rest of my days. Standing here before you, I would be greatly remiss if I didn't recognize two people in the audience. The first being my mother, who by the way reached the tender young age of ninety-three last week. Though she has been a dynamo all her life, lately her stamina, or lack there-of, will prevent her from attending this evenings dinner. Therefore I would be remiss if I did not publicly honor this woman. It was by having her as a role-model that I based my life. Her words, "Live each day to the fullest; love each day you live; live with dignity, and never be able to say you didn't do your best" have centered me, guided me and have helped me overcome adversity all my life. Mom, please stand to be recognized."

The audience responded enthusiastically to Professor Alderage-Gates request.

"Mom, thank you, thank you for everything. I love you.

"Sitting right next to my mom is a woman who has been my partner, my rock, soul-mate and best friend for the last twenty-five years, Rose Ann Tedico. When things were tough, she eased my mind. When I ranted and expressed my frustrations, she eased me back to reality. When I was imprisoned with objectivity, she balanced me out with subjectivity. Rose Ann will be with my mom this evening, therefore will also not be available for this evening's festivities. Rose Ann would you please stand up to be recognized.

"Mom, Rose Ann would you please remain standing for a moment so I can publicly acknowledge the two most important people in my life."

As Nan Alderage-Gates began to clap her hands the audience began to join in, and within a few additional seconds it seemed as if the entire field-house exploded in applause.

As the ovation began to wane, with tears streaming down from Nan, her mother and Rose Ann's eyes, Professor Earl Starkvisor arose from his seat on the rostrum, strode over to the podium, offered his arm to escort Nan Alderage-Gates to her seat. She looked down on him, and with a teary-eyed smile took his arm, turned back to acknowledge the audience and together went back to their seats.

Not wanting to allow this special moment to get lost, the Provost began to speak.

"Ladies and Gentlemen, What makes this university great is not only our being on the cutting edge of technology, our diverse and brilliant student body, our physical plant and our outstanding faculty. It is also the humanity, the sensitivity, and the respect we as a community live by. I am proud to be associated with Brookside university.

Once again the audience began to cheer.

Last and far from least, it is my pleasure to present to you **Professor Stewart Gill.**

A five foot ten inch man, weighing close to one hundred and eighty-five pounds, casually to carelessly dressed, confidently walked up to the podium.

Professor Gill is tenured in and a full-professor in I.F.S.D., the college of International Facility for Students who are Deaf. I.F.S.D. is unique in post-secondary education, for as a college, it offers no programs, nor degrees. But the almost three thousand students who are deaf and registered through I.F.S.D. at *Brookside University* would not have the rate of success they have without the interpreting services, note-taking services, tutoring services, counseling and a myriad of other services provided by the faculty and staff of I.F.D.S. Their motto is every student, especially students who are deaf, needs to have an equal playing field to become everything they can be, if they choose to be. We will make it an equal playing field!"

Each of the colleges of the university has an office within that college housed by I.F.S.D. faculty who are experts in the disciplines taught in that college. These talented men and woman teach a half load or more in the college, and at the same time supply the necessary support to students who are deaf, and being educated within that college. These faculty work five days a week, twelve months a year. I can attest to the fact that a more devoted faculty does not exist anywhere.

But now let me talk about the man, Professor Stewart Gill. In a day and age of specialization, here we find a man not only a jack-of-all-trades, but a master-of-all-trades as well. The diversity of his background is startling. And although he is a devoted, and more times than not, an out-spoken advocate for the students he represents, no one seems to mind. Where some faculty have difficulty attempting to integrate into the greater university, he is welcomed, truly an amazing feat.

His popularity is an enigma, because Professor Gill at times can be harsh. He is an idealist, who never tires of fighting university windmills. He can be heard down the hall from his office chewing out a student, deaf or hearing, who cut a class, or missed an assignment, or be found barging into a Dean's, Provost or President's office without an appointment to advocate for a student he believed had gotten a raw deal.

"But it is his diverse experience in the business world that separates him from most of his colleagues. During his tenure at *Brookside,* he has been asked to, and taught twenty six different classes at six of the colleges of the University, while fulfilling his responsibility to I.F.S.D, working with students who are deaf."

Once again the entire field house erupted, people cheering, clapping their hands and a large number of people simply waving their hands above their heads. In response Professor Gill held up his hands palms out, and almost immediately the crown noise died down.

Informing the interpreter he would be signing for himself, he effortlessly, began to sign and speak at the same time. First explaining to the audience that to many people who are deaf, waving their hands in front of them means the same as a people who are hearing clapping their hands

Then he thanked the audience for their generous support, turning to the Provost he thanked the university for opening it's doors to people who are deaf, and giving them an opportunity of not only proving themselves, but of gaining the necessary tools to earn a living, and be able to live a life of choice in a highly technological world.

As he turned to leave the provost asked him to stay, then requested Professor MacKeon, Professor Starkvisor and Professor Alderage-Gates to join Professor Gill at the podium.

"Ladies and gentlemen, here they are, Brookside University's 2009 P. Miller Annual Award recipients for Outstanding Teaching."

It took about seven minutes before the Provost was able regain control over the audience.

"Yes, these four professors are very, very special, but I would be remiss in my duties if I didn't recognize the rest of our faculty. I believe there is no finer group of educators in the world than the faculty-at-large here at Brookside University.

"To that end I would like all members of our faculty who are in attendance to stand and be recognized."

Slowly from all sections of the enormous field house, one-by-one, faculty began to rise. As they did, the applause began for a second time, equally as strong. All-in-all, more than four-hundred, full-time faculty were in attendance. It was their way of paying homage to their colleagues.

"Before closing, I would like to remind you again of the awards dinner this evening. At that dinner each of the recipients will be receiving a citation reading,

"Brookside University's, P. Miller's Annual Award for Outstanding Teaching is awarded to _____ in recognition of conspicuous success in the enhancement of teaching and learning. The award conveys the high respect and admiration of the university community."

"In addition to the citation each faculty person will receive a medallion signifying excellence in teaching, and as a distinguished member of an exclusive fraternity of educators. The medallion was designed by the late Hans Christianson, one of the foremost silversmiths in our nation, as well as a member of our faculty. It is our hope that these medallions will be worn with pride at all university functions.

"At this evening's dinner you will have the opportunity to hear in greater detail from our award recipients, as well as from the Vice President of the United States. Not many people know it, but he began his distinguished career as an educator. By the way, did I mention that there are still a few tickets available, and they can be purchased in the lobby on your way out.

"Did I forget anything? Oh yes, each award recipient will receive a check for five-thousand dollars.

"Thank you for your trust in allowing us to educate your sons and daughters. Thank you for your support, and Thank you for your energy. God Bless"

Book One
Stan MacKeon

May 20, 2007

Huntington Apartments

(A motel built in the 60's converted into studio apartments within walking distance to the university).

In the living room part of his studio apartment Stan MacKeon was sitting in his favorite chair, a big overstuffed, brown and yellow tweed armchair, with his feet resting upon a matching foot stool, sipping on his favorite beer, Labatt's Blue, and becoming nostalgic. For years now, he had been thinking of buying one of those recliners, but each time he sat in one it felt strange and vacuous; not coming close to giving him the comfort of his armchair and stool, the only link he had to his past, and his short and tempestuous married life.

"What a day this has been, and it is not over yet."

He thought it was nice to be recognized, but as rewarding as it was, it was equally exhausting.

"If this is what stardom is, I don't want it."

Tossing off his shoes, one-by-one to the other side of the room, an exercise he had become quite adept at doing. He then snuggled back into his chair, wiggled his toes, took a deep swig of his beer and let his mind wander.

"I wonder how Helen is doing ?" God, he had loved her at one time. Well, he thought he did, no he really did, at least in the beginning. All five foot, nine inches of her. All one-hundred and sixty pounds of her. Her fire-red hair dangling loose about her shoulders. That white translucent skin. The subtle freckles around her nose and upper cheek bones. Oh how she hated them, and oh how he had loved to tease her about them.

"It would have been nice to have her here to share this day with. But I guess it just wasn't meant to be."

As he began to romanticize, the reality of their relationship reared its ugly head.

"God, why did it happen to me, her, yes, her too, to be fair. Looking back at it now she was as much a victim as he. Catholic guilt, and that bitch nun...I could have killed her, maybe I should have. No, I doubt it would have changed a thing. Shit happens. You live and then you die. Schopenhauer was right."

His memory, renowned to be almost photographic, began to replay for him, one after another, of the past unpleasant experiences of their lives together. He loved his ability to recall almost anything, but lately that same ability was driving him to drink vast amounts of brew, even faster than before. In doing so, his melancholy was beginning to consume him sooner and sooner, something he was going to have to watch.

✵

Helen Ann Maguire.

December 1959

St. Ignacio's, the largest church, and parochial school in the area, was located on West Street, just north of Berrigan's Road. This was Irish Town with lots of one and two-family asbestos-shingled boxes, people politely called homes. Block after block, there were red-brick and white brick row houses, most in dis-repair, which earlier-on were the homes of upper and middle-class folk who moved out of the city. Now these domiciles have become rooming houses and tenement apartments to the never-ending immigrant families arriving, seemingly daily. Remnants of this once lovely area were one or two tired, drooping maple trees waiting to die. Though the area was not technically a slum, many who populated the area were very casual with their garbage.

The Maguire's, consisted of Patsy, Shannon, and their four children. Devon, the eldest at sixteen, Patrick two years younger and the twins Elizabeth and Helen now almost thirteen all lived on the second floor of a two story house located at 2234 Center Street.

The twins, Elizabeth and Helen, though identical, were as far different as possible. Elizabeth, technically the oldest by seven minutes, was just like her dad in every aspect except looks. She was fun loving, loved to tell jokes and entertain the regulars at MacKeon's bar when her father let her accompany him on Friday evenings. At thirteen years of age the twins were almost as tall as their father. They were solidly build, had bright red hair, white skin, pretty as a postcard, and could and would deck any boy who upset them.

Helen felt alien from her family. She was a very serious student at school, impressing the Sisters with her ability to learn and her devotion to God. She loved St Ignacio's, where Elizabeth hated it. She would get upset when her brothers and parents swore at home, but was not able to express herself. The more the members of her family drank, the more, and louder the swearing became. She hated it when her mother, after preparing dinner on Friday, told the girls that she was going to meet dad at MacKeon's for a pint. Knowing the next time she would see her mother was when her parents, drunk as skunks would struggle up the stairs and barely make it to their bedroom.

Elizabeth was sensing that Helen and she were drifting apart; something that never happened before. They always had their differences, but they were usually trivial ones. Now Helen was separating herself from the family, seemingly at every opportunity, and worst of all, was averse to talk about it.

It was just after six pm, Friday evening, a week before Christmas. Mrs. Maguire was preparing stew for dinner, the boys, having come home about an hour ago were lounging around tuned into *WIRM*, the so called Irish station, and Elizabeth was contemplating escorting her father to MacKeon's to be spoiled rotten by Dad's friends, possibly do a song or two, and just maybe her own version of an Irish jig. Helen was sitting at the table in the kitchen already attacking her homework. "Jesus to Mary" (an expression Elizabeth heard her father say a lot) Hellie, "you have all weekend for that. School's over for the week, thank God! Now put that stuff away and let's practice some carols before Dad comes home."

"No, I can't. Sister Caroline wants us to write a report on Christmas and Literature. She refused to explain any more. She said it is up to us to interpret her meaning, and have enough confidence in ourselves to risk being wrong. I can't be wrong. You know how important it is for me to be right. I'm so frustrated, I am ready to cry."

Elizabeth knew if she didn't do something quickly, the entire weekend would be shot. The boys, as usual would start teasing Helen, mocking her seriousness, Sister Caroline and St. Ignacio's. Helen would start to cry, and the boys would do what boys do, intensify their teasing, Helen would add screaming to her crying, and would plead with her Mom, "do something Ma, make them stop! Mom would attempt to establish some quiet, by threatening all with 'the stick" if order was not immediately restored, knowing that if Dad walked into the fray, all hell will break out.

At that very moment Dad came barging into the apartment with a smile as big as Copley Square. "Gather round me fine folk, look what your Dad has." In his hand, an envelope with two ten dollar bills and a five showing. "Mr. Cordon my boss, came up to me at closing time while I was cleaning my hands. Hands me this envelope, tells me how glad he is that I work for him; that I'm doing a great job, never a complaint, and to show his appreciation hands me this envelope and says, Merry Christmas, and to give his good wishes to all of you. He's never done that before, so you know it got to be a good Christmas. So I decided to start the holiday off right, after dinner I'm taking the whole family to MacKeon's for a celebration. What do you think of that?"

Hearing their father come home, the boys ventured forth, and when Dad began extolling his good fortune they started cheering, for if Dad was happy, everyone would be too. Mom gushing with pride ran up to Dad and began to smother him with hugs and kisses. Elizabeth, knowing Helen was in one of "her" moods grabbed Helen's arm, pulled her up from her seat and propelled her to her father. Nothing or no one would ruin this evening.

Right after setting the table Elizabeth took Helen aside, and told her not to worry. She had a plan. Each occasion she had been to MacKeon's with Dad, she saw a tall young man sitting at a table in the back reading. Asking Mr. MacKeon who that person was, "my son, Lizzie, my son. Do me a favor girl, go up to him and say hi. He is a good boy, but all he does is read, read, read, and then tell anyone who will listen about what he has read."

I did, and he looked up at me smiled. "You're Elizabeth Maguire aren't you. Your Dad is a regular here, and I've seen you with him a few times. Have a seat if you'd like." Then he offered me some of his beer and started to tell me about the book he was reading. I smiled back and told him thank you, but no thank you, but I have a twin sister who would love to meet you. He smiled a very gentle smile back to me and said, "bring her down, why don't you, I'm always here.

MacKeon's was a typical local tavern. Upon entering, to the right was a huge, dark-brown wooden bar with a thick, grey-marble counter extending the entire length of the place, featuring in the middle, six different taps serving up six different Irish beers and ales. The bar was so large it could accommodate at least 20 bar stools with sufficient space between them for twenty standing people. At any hour of the day, at least half a dozen men clustered in two or three groups, could be found discussing not much of anything and sipping their pints. If they weren't such good customers they would have had to pay rent.

Behind the bar attached to the wall were three etched glass shelves laden with a huge array of liquors, beer mugs and a variety of glasses of different sizes and shapes. On the walls covering almost all the wall space were posters of Ireland, Irish pubs, and of people having a grand old time in the pubs. The few bare spots between posters were taken up by neon signs depicting the names of different Irish brews. The rest of the tavern was filled with twelve round wooden tables with six matching seats, an old fashioned juke box, a small supply cabinet, and two bathrooms.

The Maguire's had just entered the premises, all six of them.

"The whole family is it? What's the occasion?"

"Got me a nice bonus from my boss, and tis the season my friend, tis the season."

By 7:30pm on Friday evening MacKeon's was usually three quarters full. On this evening, one week before Christmas it was even more crowded. Patsy Maguire, after greeting a dozen or so friends, located a table for his family. *Dennis Day*, Mr. MacKeon's favorite Irish tenor (he had every record the tenor recorded) was playing on the juke box, accompanied by one customer playing the harmonica, and another on the accordion. People were talking, laughing, and just having a jolly time. The mood being infectious, the Maguire's were soon part of the festivities, that is all but one, Helen. Her parents, the boys and Elizabeth were table-hopping, touching base with the locals, and simply glad to be alive. Being the first time both twins were present, they were the talk of the crowd.

"My God Patty, look at them, identical beauties. How'd you do it?" "Stunning I say, stunning!"

Elizabeth, eating up the attention while imbibing a sip or two from the good neighbor's glasses, noticed at the back of the room a tall young man alternating between reading a book and looking at her. As their eyes made contact he gave her a smile. Her first reaction was one of coyness, then she remembered her plan. She ran over to the table Helen was morosely and stiffly sitting at, and literally pulled her sister across the room to where Stan MacKeon was sitting.

"Remember me, I'm Elizabeth Maguire?"

"How could I forget a young lady as lovely as you are."

"Cut the blarney won't you, while smiling and blushing at the same time. I told you I thought you would enjoy meeting my sister. I'd like to introduce you to Helen Maguire, the smart one in the family."

"I know I've only had three, well maybe four beers, but I swear you must be carrying a mirror and trying to make a fool of me. You are the spitting image of each other, Elizabeth one, and Elizabeth two."

"My name is Helen, and I am not a mirror image of my sister, nor am I a mirror image of anyone. I'm flesh and blood, and to prove it I will allow you touch my hand, here!"

As Stan MacKeon reached out to take hand, Helen quickly drew back." I told you, Mr. MacKeon, you could touch my hand, not hold it!"

"Sorry, I didn't mean to offend you, but if I did, I apologize, and please do me a favor, just call me Stan."

Elizabeth once again knew it was up to her to save the day.

"Okay, Stan, my sister Helen here, is in need of some assistance, and I thought you might be the perfect person to help her. As I mentioned to you before, Helen is the bright one, she loves books, it's fine for her, but in my opinion she is much too serious about her studies. She was given an assignment in school today that is worrying her. You see she has this need to excel, and I can't help her. If you could, you would be doing a true Christian deed."

With that Elizabeth did a spin and disappeared into the now standing-room only crowd. Helen, standing as stiff as a mannequin didn't move. So Stan MacKeon rose, pulled out the chair next to him, and invited Helen to sit down.

"Why don't you tell me what the assignment is. I'm sure I can be of assistance."

At first Helen had trouble concentrating. Stan MacKeon was to her eyes the most handsome person she had ever seen. Standing 5'9" tall, she wasn't used to being with boys taller than her. And he was, had to be at least 6'2", she later found out he was almost 6'3".

"Can I get you something to drink?"

Hearing something being said, Helen was stunned out of her revelry. "What, what was that you said?"

"I said, can I get you anything to drink? Soda, beer, Irish whiskey?"

Flustered, unable to utter anything more than "ah, ah," and "oh," She felt she had to momentarily close her eyes to regain a modicum of control.

"No, no, no thank you, I don't, don't drink. I mean, I don't drink alcohol, I do drink pop, and hot tea, and milk, and…other things. It's not only that I am too young to drink, but I think it sinful, and all my teachers agree with me."

"Where do you attend school, and by the way, how old are you anyway?"

"I go to St. Ignacio's, and, and I am thirteen years old."

"That explains it."

"Explains what?"

"Your age girl, your age, you are a mere child. Granted no one would believe it looking at you."

"Stop that, and stop looking at me like that! I am no mere child. I can do anything I want to do. If I wanted to take a drink of alcohol I could, I Just don't want to. I've seen what it does to people. My parents come home from here, and sometimes can barely make it up the steps. My brothers, after a night of drinking, usually pass out on the bathroom floor after throwing up their guts. And who do you think has to clean up after them?"

"Helen, please, please sit down. I didn't mean anything wrong. I was not making fun of you. I like you. I like your energy, and when you get upset your eyes sparkle. If I said anything to offend you, I'm sorry. Now please tell me about your school assignment."

The rest of the evening the two of them sat in the back of the bar, discussing at first literature, then their personal histories, their likes and dislikes. Only when the bar was closing, and Elizabeth was sent to fetch her sister, did the conversation come to an end. The fact that he was five years older than she, made no difference at all. They were kindred spirits. In due time, Stan MacKeon suggested to Helen that her teacher was not trying to trick her, but merely extending an open-ended opportunity to express what Christmas meant to her via the books she chose, and the conclusions she made based on the meanings she attributed to the story. He suggested two authors and works; *The Gift of the Magi*, a short story by O'Henry, and *A Christmas Carol* by Charles Dickens. She replied that she had read *A Christmas Carol*, liked it very much, and could see how it could work on her report, but was not familiar with O'Henry. Since he had a copy of O'Henry's short stories at home, he suggested they meet there at the bar the next morning. He had to be there anyway since it was his responsibility to clean up, and if she'd like, they could have some time to discuss ideas as to the paper she was to write. At first she looked away, and said she wasn't sure, but when he asked why she had no answer. She felt stuck. After all Helen went to a all girl's school, and other than her two rotten brothers, and a father who drank too much, she had no experience with boys. Not being able to think of one reason, she took a deep breath, looked back at him, and agreed to meet him.

Armed with confidence that a man as smart as Stan MacKeon would be helping her, and more importantly, that she was more than a tad smitten with the man, Helen left MacKeon's with her family, but would swear her feet never touched the pavement on the walk home.

Helen Ann Maguire.

December 1963

Since meeting at MacKeon's the week before Christmas four years before, they had managed to see each other almost every week. Usually their liaisons were on Saturday mornings, when they could be alone in the bar, and on Sunday's on her way home from church. Since no one in the family joined her for Mass, Helen was free to do what she wanted, and what she wanted was to spend time with Stan.

In the beginning of their relationship, she sat and listened while Stan did the talking, mostly about the books he read and was currently reading. She loved hearing his voice. He made each book sound like a fantasy. Helen would shut her eyes, and let his words transport her to some exotic time or place. And then at the appropriate time, somehow he always knew when, he would stop reading or talking and begin to question her to make sure she understood what the story was about. Then when he was sure she understood, he would begin reading again.

Within the year, as she became more confident, she would not wait for him to ask if she needed clarification of some aspect of the story, or the meaning of some word, she merely interrupted his reading and posed the question. Then as her confidence continued to grow, she began to offer her opinions.

By the second year of their relationship, they had to agree to take turns, for both enjoyed being the leader. Helen would sit in Stan's regular seat, and he in hers, then begin by discussing one of the books they had previously discussed, but now Helen was the teacher. Stan loved it almost as much as Helen did. There she would stand (she didn't like reading aloud while being seated) throw her shoulders back, chin up and start performing. He couldn't take his eyes off of her. Helen was not only growing taller, but was filling out and looking more like a woman than a girl. When the book discussion ended, they would talk about what happened or didn't happen in school. Then share their plans for the upcoming week. Then Stan would need to begin attending to his chores in the bar, and Helen would head home to complete her chores and homework. Within two months of their start-up, Stan escorted Helen to the door holding her hand, the same one she pulled away from him that first night. She didn't remember when it started, but at some point before she could exit, he had bent over and planted a small kiss on her cheek. She had looked up at him, smiled, said good bye, and disappeared into the street. From that time on, she never left without her good-by kiss.

Helen had never been happier. She had found a kindred spirit, not only a kindred spirit, but a tall, handsome, polite one, who treated her with respect and dignity. Though they differed on a number of, what would become important issues, they had each other, and life in the neighborhood was good.

The MacKeon's

Successfully defending himself two or three times at the beginning of each academic year in the school yard enabled Stan to fend off peer pressure to involve himself in sports. Just because he was tall and strong did not mean he was athletic. He simply did not enjoy sports; had nothing in common with boys, and not having much social experience was very awkward with girls. Stan simply shied away from people in general.

Since his mother had died, he spent most of his time in the bar with his Dad, either being helpful or trying to be invisible. Other than Friday and Saturday nights, MacKeon's was basically patronized by men, older Irish men, the same older Irish men. So Stan would bury himself in the back and read until it was close-up time, then accompany his father home. Seven days a week, every week.

Danny MacKeon was a good, kind and gentle man. A man who adored his wife, as well as a man who was a good provider. Since Stan was an only child, and his mother worked side-by-side with his father, the decision was made to take a small amount of space away from the supply room and construct a wall with a window and door. A room in which the lad could be kept out of harm's way, as well as provide a space for the boy to entertain himself. Stan could then look out and see his parents, and they could look in on him any time.

The space, approximately seven feet by nine feet, was initially furnished with a crib, a small dresser, a standing lamp and some toys. As he grew, the crib was converted to a bed. The dresser replaced by a play table and a small chair. It didn't take long, since Stan was growing like a weed, for his small bed to replaced by a day bed; the play table and small chair was replaced by an old roll-top desk accompanied by a chair that would adjust to Stan's rapid growth, and a lamp that he could read by. Customers knew the space was off-limits to all but Stan's parents. In fact, Stan's father meticulously lettered, "Stan the Man's Room" on the door, right above, "Keep Out!"

Slightly into his eighth year, Stan's mother became very ill, and most of her days were spent in excruciating pain. Try as they may, the doctors could not determine the cause, nor find a cure. Within six months she mercifully passed away in her sleep. His father was devastated.

After the wake, which everyone in the neighborhood attended, Stan announced to his father he was no longer in need of his special space. He planned to work side-by-side with his father. And so the walls came down, the furniture found a new home in the cellar, and Stan was on his way towards adulthood.

Tending bar was out of the question, and so he assumed the responsibility for cleaning up at closing time. His job was to make sure the bathrooms were clean and equipped, as well as washing and stacking the glasses. Since he was big for his age, all he needed was a wooden crate to stand on to accomplish that task, and any other general, menial tasks he could handle.

Though not outwardly affectionate, Stan knew that his father loved him dearly as did he loved his father. Yet, since the funeral, he sensed a certain sadness and a loneliness in his father. Wanting to ease his father's pain, Stan tried everything he knew to make his father happy.

Looking at his son with loving eyes, and not knowing what he could do, his father would simply smile at him, muss up his hair, and tell him to find a chair in the back of the bar, and keep himself busy.

This was the time Stan's love affair with literature began.

Over the years he developed a voracious appetite for books, and the public library became his second home. The librarian, Mrs. Doubleday, began to notice this young man returning the three books he borrowed every three days, and didn't know what to make of it. Becoming a little suspicious, one afternoon she approached him as he was returning the books, and engaged him in a conversation about the content of the books he was returning. Not only did he answer her with insight far beyond his years, but he appeared to relish the opportunity to talk about them. Within the month she was convinced this was a special young man, and not only told him he could borrow six books at a time, and that she would find time in her schedule to discuss his reading on a weekly basis. As their relationship grew, their discussions went beyond the books he was reading, and included his plans for the future, and aspects of his home-life.

Plans? He had no plans other than working in the bar with his Dad. When he became of legal age to dispense liquor, he would take over that responsibility from his Dad, well maybe not take over, but at least share it. He proudly told her how he was able to hook up the kegs under to bar to the taps that dispensed the beer. A task he loved, for he had to make sure each tap functioned properly. So whatever beer or ale that was dispensed in the testing process, he would make sure was not wasted. You see he was taught at a young age, "waste not, want not." And so he consumed the liquid. He was wearing a broad grin when he explained there were six taps.

One day during her lunch hour Mrs. Doubleday walked over to MacKeon's Bar and Grill. It was a beautiful day, the sun was shining, and the air refreshing. She had been planning to take this trip for a while, just never got around to it. But after last week's discussion, knew she could no longer put it off.

She had no problem finding the bar and grill. Entering the premises, she immediately recognized Stan's face on the older man behind the bar. In her matter-of-fact manner, she walked up to him, introduced herself and declared she was here to speak to him about his son. The man behind the bar gave her a quizzical look, dried his hands with the bar towel, and said, "Are you talking about Stanley Purvis MacKeon, because if you are, yes he is my son? Is he in any trouble"

"Oh, no, no, no. Stan, is one of the nicest young men I have ever had the privilege to meet. I apologize if I gave you a start. My name is Doris Doubleday. I am the head librarian at the *South End Memorial Library* down at Dorchester and Dover Streets. She then explained that in her opinion Stan was a very gifted young man. Was he aware of that fact?

No, he didn't know his son had a special gift. Yes, he knew about Stan's reading habits, but never put the two together. Looking Doris Doubleday right in her eyes, standing there prim and proper, as erect as an arrow, he said to himself, "she's not Irish, but I'll bet she is one tough package." As his guard came down, he came out from behind the bar, and guided Mrs. Doubleday to a table. Then began to answer her questions about Stan's history.

Within minutes three of the regulars seated at the bar started to demand refills, and some conversation. "Sorry Mrs. Doubleday, I have to cut our conversation short. After all, business is business."

"Of course I understand, but before I leave I need to ask you one last question. "Can I have your permission to guide your son's reading habits? I would like to introduce him to more adult books, but in doing so, I would also be introducing him to some of the seedier sides of life, and to adult themes. "

Mr. MacKeon responded by saying the sooner the boy became the man the better off he would be. It was a tough world out there. So she had his blessings. "Before you leave I would like to thank you for your interest in my son, for the encouragement you have given him, and for the assistance you will give him in the future. With that they shook hands, and she departed. Mr. MacKeon returned to his usual location behind the bar to try to appease the regulars. Before her shoes hit the pavement she was making up a variety of reading lists.

After finishing high school, Stan's reading habits didn't change, but in her opinion the quality of the books he was choosing for himself was not to her liking. The weekly discussions became monthly. He explained to her his world was expanding, and he was now working full-time at his father's bar and grill. All true, and while he still enjoyed the time with Mrs. Doubleday, they were no longer as challenging, nor as special as they once were.

Sensing this young man was starting to drift, she knew she would lose him, and the world would lose a potential scholar if something was not done, and done soon. Over a year out of high school, already comfortable in the bar with his father, consuming more of the spirits than she believed was in his best interests, and speaking to her of this young lady he was seeing, were all signs that he was at a critical period in his life.

The previous week she received in the mail a copy of the *Cosmopolitan, New York University's* alumni newsletter. The article which caught her interest was about the upcoming plans to celebrate the 40th anniversary of the university's *Ralph Waldo Emerson's Scholarship in English Literature.* Plans were being made for a two day program, in which ten of the former recipients of the scholarship, including a Poet Laureate, a Pulitzer Prize winner, three of the best selling novelists in this country, and two Professor Emeriti would be on the program. Though she herself was not an *Emerson Scholar,* her favorite teacher, Professor Richard Greene was. She recalled how he could make the telephone book sound interesting. And for years after graduating she could still call upon him for guidance or an objective opinion.

Stan MacKeon reminded her a great deal of Professor Greene. A little taller, and not as stout, but both with more than a touch of the blarney, the blarney only talented story tellers have.. "I wonder if that was what drew me to both the man, and then the boy? Hmmm, interesting" she mused.

She had lost touch with the professor almost a decade ago after years of casual correspondence. Saying to herself this would not only be a great opportunity to get reacquainted, but also to talk with him and get some advice about what to do about Stan MacKeon.

Richard Greene was impressed. After listening to two audio tapes Mrs. Doubleday recorded of their last two discussions (without Stan's knowledge), and reading four reports Stan had written for her, he agreed with Mrs. Doubleday that this was a special young man.

"His insight and clarity of Gide's *The Immoralist* is extraordinary; what high school student knows, and for that matter understands Existentialism? And his empathy for Thomas Mann's hero in *A Death in Venice* exposes in the lad a heart of a lover. This sophistication is far beyond this young man's years. Why, I have graduate students majoring in English Literature that don't have his grasp of the subject matter. It is readily apparent this boy has special talents, but why are you expending so much effort on the boy's behalf, Doris?'

Her face reddening, she closed her eyes and said: "Since I was a student in your classes, I developed a great affection for you Professor Greene. Your classes literally changed my life. Adrift, not knowing what I was going to do with my life, your passion and sheer joy for literature was so infectious, I knew then that this was the path I would pursue. It has been a wonderful life, and I thank you for being you. To address your question directly, I believe this young man has the gifts to be able to become a scholar, and effect others in the same manner you effected me. Gifted teachers who are also gifted scholars do not come along every day." As the last word exited her mouth, her face almost beet red, she was finally able to look up at her mentor.

"Thank you Doris. I've been paid compliments before, but none have been more elegant and warm sounding as yours. I'll tell you what, I will arrange for a scholarship application packet to be sent to you. Have the young lad fill out the general admissions application as well as the special application for the *Emerson scholarship*. He will need to include three letters of recommendation, excluding mine, a transcript of his grades, a three thousand word essay entitled, "The role of literature in this century", and lastly, a one hundred dollar application fee.

Upon completion, check the entire package. Make sure every "i" is dotted, and every "t" is crossed. Then return it to directly to me, not the admissions office. If everything is in order, and the information bears out your confidence, I will personally steer it to the right people. Your job will be to guide him well. If you do your job, and I am as capable as I think I am, you just might have the next Richard Greene on your hands. He was beaming as a new father, and she was tingling all over.

"Stan, good to see you, sorry I missed our discussion last month, but I had a schedule conflict. It was alumni week at N.Y.U. and I couldn't miss it."

"No problem Mrs. Doubleday, I mean, I missed talking to you, but when you gotta do something, you just gotta do it."

"Please sit down, I have something I want to discuss with you. Hear me out, and I hope you won't be upset with me. Please don't say anything, just listen. I had an alternative reason for going to New York. Part of the festivities was the 40th anniversary of the *Ralph Waldo Emerson's Scholarship in English Literature.* On the program was one of my old teachers, Richard Greene. He is not only one of the most gifted teachers at the university, but is known across the world for his critiques and commentaries on new and old literature.

A while back I spoke to your Dad, and asked him for permission to introduce you to more complex and controversial literature. As a minor, I had no choice. You were getting bogged down in the same themes, and books that, how can I put it, books that did nothing for you. After a long talk, he agreed to allow me to guide you towards more sophisticated reading, and thanked me for any past and future guidance I have bestowed upon you..

Granted, that was a few years ago, but I took it as his blessing to explore ways for you to continue to grow, and hopefully begin to fulfill your potential.

To that end, without your knowledge, I taped the last two sessions we had on *Gide* and *Mann*. I played them for Professor Greene then showed him the last four papers you wrote for me.

To say he was impressed would be an understatement. He sent me this packet of materials, and volunteered to write a letter of recommendation for you. The packet contains the standard application papers for entrance into *New York University*, and additional papers applying for the *Ralph Waldo Emerson Scholarship in English Literature.* Only one recipient per year is awarded a scholarship that covers full tuition, room and board, books and fees for four years.

I think it is important you understand that *New York University* has one of the most respected Language and Literature Departments in the world, and the *Emerson Scholarship* is in my estimation the most coveted scholarship there is in the field of Literature. It not only means the student who is awarded the scholarship will get, as it is called in academia, "a free-ride", but far more importantly it is as close to a guarantee that the student will have his/her choice of graduate schools anywhere in the world to pursue graduate and post-graduate studies.

Now, there are no guarantees, but with Richard Greene supporting you behind the scenes, I would feel pretty good about your chances. "

Stan did not know what to say.

He had not really given the future much thought. His life was set. MacKeon's Bar and Grill was his world. He and his father spent seven days a week there. Five days a week they went to work, and came home together. On weekends, he would arrive early to clean the residue of the past night's frolicking and prepare for the upcoming night's cheer. This gave his father a little more time to rest, and him some private time.

He loved the weekends.

Helen would arrive a little after nine, and sit on one of the stools in the back and watch him complete his chores. Then Stan would proceed to the table Helen was sitting at, and they would begin to share with each other the joy and excitement of the books they had read that week, interspersed with the events the week had provided them.

Around noon-time Mr. MacKeon would arrive, see them in the back of the bar and wave. Helen feeling these men were more her family then her family would respond, "Good morning, or should I say good afternoon Mr. MacKeon."

"And a glorious good morning, or be it afternoon to you Helen." Grinning from ear to ear the father answered back, "make no mind of me, I'll just be doing what a working stiff has to do to keep this bar afloat, and my son on the straight and narrow. By the way, is he treating you right? He better be, or I'll take the strap to him. A gentleman he will be, that is the MacKeon way."

This repartee had become standard fare by now, after all Stan and Helen have been seeing each other in this manner for about two years, and Dad's presence would signal it was time for her to depart. Nevertheless, they both eagerly looked forward to this time of the week. Their being together seemed as natural as peas in a pod.

But in this world, innocence is only a temporary condition.

Since neither dated nor saw anyone else, Stan now a healthy, hearty young man, couldn't help but to begin to recognize more and more that this charming, adorable young miss had grown into a vivacious young woman.

Helen's naiveté, and physicality was beginning to impact on Stan's objectivity. Content to be so happy she would throw her arms around him, and hug him, while his good-bye kisses, and farewell embraces would linger and be firmer.

Now at her full height, 5'9", her silken-red hair hung in ringlets two inches below her shoulders, while her skin glowed an alabaster white, dabbled with the subtlest freckles of light-honey on her cheeks and nose. Her figure, earlier on, almost cylindrical, now had taken on more of an hour-glass shape.

As facile as he was with the English language, and as charming a conversationalist as he was with customers, over the last six months or so, Stan was finding he was having more and more trouble expressing himself to Helen. Recently, each time she hugged and/or kissed him his body began to stir. The aroma of her innocence, the touch of her skin and the perfection of her body was short-circuiting his ability to listen, as well as think. Try as he may he could not put a stop to these feelings.

Over the course of recent weeks Helen had noticed he was not as attentive as he always had been. More than once she found herself repeating two, sometimes three times, a simple thought. She also noticed recently that a stammer had entered his voice, and while not being rude, he was looking away from her more and more. She knew in her heart something had to be wrong. What had she done? Was it something she said?

The clock read 12:15, fifteen minutes later than her usual departure time. But the fear of having to live a week with the dire possibilities that were racing through her mind that their relationship was in trouble overcame her hesitancy to ask: "Stan, is there anything wrong? Lately you haven't been acting like yourself. Is it something I have done?" As her voice receded into silence, tears began to cascade down over her cheeks.

Watching her speak, seeing tears flowing down her cheeks, knowing he was responsible, he acted without thinking. He rushed to her side, engulfed her in his arms while caressing her hair, and assured her nothing was wrong. Being in each others arms seemed as natural to both as breathing. The minutes they were together seemed an eternity. As they began to part, Stan bent over and engaged her lips passionately.

"I'm so sorry Helen. I don't know what has gotten into me. I, I...

Helen looked at him, at first confused and surprised, then slowly smiled and said it was okay. Still in his arms she reached up and kissed him back, then whispered in his ear, "I've dreamed of this for almost a year."

"What's going on there?" A voice bellowed from the front of the room.

"Nothing Dad, we were just saying good-bye."

"Alright then, get on with it. We have work to do."

Walking her to the front door, he whispered, "I'll see you tomorrow, I can't wait."

"Me too", she whispered back.

Over the course of the next few months, words of love became partnered with passionate kissing. Encouraged by her sister

Elizabeth (who just happened to be dating three high school seniors and three college freshmen at the time) to experiment and seek life out to its fullest, Helen let Stan touch her breast over her sweater. It was an act so electrifying, its shock waves immobilized both for the moment. Discovering the real thing far exceeded anything his imagination had invented, Stan attempted to explore more of Helens body. When kissing, his tongue probed Helen's mouth. At first she resisted, but the feelings she was experiencing soon weakened her will, and she soon found herself an equally aggressive participant.

Within a short time their weekend book review, general discussion sessions and critiques quickly moved to passionate kissing and heavy petting. Then one Sunday twenty minutes into their groping, Stan put his hand under her sweater and into her bra touching her nipple. Helen reacted as if he had smacked her.

"No, don't, I can't. It's wrong. Oh my God, what are we doing?" Having disengaged from his arms, she backed away from him. This is all wrong. We have to stop doing this, it's a sin. Sister Caroline told me this would happen. First kissing, then touching, then… you know what then. She said it was a sin, a terrible sin. The more we kiss and touch the less control I have. We can't do this any more. I went to confession yesterday. Father Kerrigan told me Sister Caroline was right. I was playing with fire, hell-fire, and only bad would come of this behavior. "

Helen's body was shaking uncontrollably, her eyes red from crying, her face contorted with pain. Trying to calm her, he attempted to hold her. "No! don't touch me!" And with that ran out of his grasp and into the street running all the way to St. Ignacio's, into the church, and started praying for forgiveness to the Holy Mother of God before her knees touched the ground.

Stan was stunned, unable to comprehend what happened. Her reaction in his mind inexplicable. Without thinking he walked behind the bar and poured himself a double shot of Irish whiskey. All it took was one swallow to consume the amber liquid, and after his body stopped shaking (he was a beer drinker) he poured himself a second, then a third, then a fourth… by the time his father showed up he was drunk out of his skull.

It took about fifteen minutes for his father to make some sense out of the gibberish coming out of his mouth. "Kiss, Helen, touch, scream, run." Once his father started to put two and two together he understood that his son and Helen were doing more than just discussing books. Clearly their relationship had moved into a new, more serious venue.

Putting a sign on the door that read, "be back in 20 minutes", Mr. MacKeon, not without a great deal of difficulty, dragged his son home, and somehow got him into bed. Knowing he would be there for quite some time, and upon awakening from his stupor, sick as a dog for the rest of the day, he looked at the picture hanging on the wall of his dear, departed wife and said out loud, "the boy's becoming a man. Yes my dear, our son is becoming a man." From time to time he had fretted over the fact that Stan never made an attempt to date any girl, nor did he go off with friends to have some fun. Even upon his urging, Stan had said he was more than content to see young Helen, and read books, and work in the bar with his father.

Walking back to the bar, he more than chuckled to himself that Mother Nature had her own time-table for doing things, and it seemed to have caught up to Stan and Helen.

Saturday morning, 10:00am.

MacKeon's Bar and Grill

Two months had elapsed without a word passing between them. Engaged in the senseless task of sweeping, his mind turned to the conversation he seemed to have with himself on a daily basis. Vacillating between being angry at himself for his crude attempt at investigating Helen's body, then rationalizing she was old enough to get married… seventeen, and more importantly she seemed to be enjoying their engagements as much as he. So why, why… for the life of him, he could not understand her total breakdown. Yes he cared for her, might even love her, but with her panic attack, and the stuff she threw at him about sinning and hell…no, he was glad it happened, not the *way* it happened, but glad it happened.

After what happened to his mother, and the forever sadness his father wore, he could not abide the church, nor the people who worked it.

On the other hand,

he really cared for Helen. The nearly four years they had been seeing each other were wonderful. They had so much in common. She was bright and grasped subtleties like no one else he knew, the same things saddened and gladdened them.

On the other hand,

her devotion to Catholicism, her need to go to church and confession: how could someone that bright, and full of spirit buy into that dogma. It made no sense to him. He believed in God all right, and he knew God was all around him and with him all the time. He didn't need a building to access God. And if we were children of God, wouldn't God want what any other parent wants for their children; to be healthy, to enjoy life and have fun?

On the other hand

when he looked at her, he thought she was the most beautiful girl on God's Earth. When they touched, it was almost as becoming one. When he held her, and kissed her his body tingled.

On the other hand…

"Stan."

He quickly turned towards the voice. "Can we talk, please, I really need to talk to you?" As he listened to her, a soft tearful voice, he saw her standing just inside the doorway, shoulders hunched, feet together, eyes red, a frightened, almost pitiable 5'9" pixie. "Please Stan, I need to talk to you. Please let me come in. I've been miserable, unable to sleep, and I can't stop crying. Please, oh please let me try to explain. I'm so confused. You are my heart and soul. I love you more than I can express in words. The last two years were the best years of my life, please…"

Without understanding the reason why, he rushed to her, embraced her and attempted to calm her down. Nothing else mattered. She was here, he was holding her, they were together again. After a bit, as if drawn by a magnet to "their" table, they sat, and simply looked at each other.

Helen was the first to speak. "I am so sorry. I don't know what came over me." He tried to say something, but she asked him to please let her say what she had to say without interruption, because she was not sure she could do it if he spoke.

"I think, no I know, I am different than anyone else in my family. And if I didn't look exactly alike as my sister, I would swear I was adopted. Because I am not comfortable with people, and love school, especially reading, my family, mostly my brothers, make fun of me. My father says he doesn't understand me, my mother looks at me with doleful eyes, and shakes her head as if saying, "dear God, why me." My sister, though kind, just doesn't understand me, and is too busy enjoying life to spend much time with me.

Sister Caroline at St. Ignacio's has been the only one I could talk to. She has been one of my teachers, seemingly forever. Knowing how well I read, she introduced me to many passages in the bible which she said would give me comfort, and they have. Before you, she was the only one who would listen to me, and take me serious, and the bible soothed my spirits when I was alone. Sister Caroline even suggested I might find a satisfying and comforting life serving the Mother Church.

A week before we, I, ran away from you, I asked to speak to Sister Caroline in private. I told her about you, about us, and how wonderful our weekends have been. When she inquired what we did when we were together, I couldn't lie to her. I told her about our book discussions, how we spoke of what was happening in the world, and in our lives, then mentioned to her how it felt holding, hugging and kissing you, that it almost felt we were one. She asked it you had touched my personal parts. I told her that you put your hand on my breast, and I also told her it felt good. And that was why I needed to talk to her.

After I got home the previous Sunday, before I ran away, I began to feel uneasy feeling so good about how close we were, and how I was beginning to feel sensations in my body I had never felt before. It frightened me, it really frightened me.

Sister Caroline told me how glad she was that I came to see her. She said I had reached a turning point in my life. She knew all about the sensations I was feeling, saying every woman has them. She said God gave them to all women when they were physically capable of child bearing. It is those sensations that primes woman's bodies for sexual intercourse and procreation. For that reason it is also the burden women must bear, for sexual activity for its own sake is a sin. Just as the snake tempted Eve in the Garden of Eden, men will attempt to lure women into intercourse with their kisses and touching. She said you must control your urges until you are married, then intercourse becomes a blessing, for the seed your husband will plant in you, eventually you will nurture, and bring forth God's greatest of all miracles, a child.

She said she had faith in me. That I was a good Catholic, and that God was proud of me. It was now up to me to stop you from taking further advantage of me. That's when I told her you never took advantage of me. Everything we did was by mutual consent. She cautioned me that might have been true in the past, but wait, I would see you would not be content with the status quo, you would want more.

I struggled and prayed all week, but it didn't help. Then when we were embraced, and your hand went under my sweater and touched my nipple, I, I, I panicked, and lost control of my senses."

Having completed her explanation, her voice faded, her eyes shifted from him to the floor, while her hands in her lap never moved.

How could he be upset with her. She was a victim. That nun from St. Ignacio's was the guilty one. Helen, as bright as she was, was still naive, that was part of her charm. It was all that religious shit that messed with her head. "Helen, I am so sorry I have caused you such turmoil. I care for you very much, in fact I think

I am in love with you. I would never do anything to hurt you. I understand why you acted the way you did. It was that Sister Caroline who messed you up. What a bitch!"

"Please Stan, don't, she's a nun."

"Okay, I won't call her a bitch, but she set you up. She played you like the young innocent you are. You did nothing wrong Helen. Innocence is good, innocence is honesty. I too am innocent. I have never been with a girl before. In fact you are the first girl I've ever touched like that. I thought if we felt the way we do about each other, we could learn and experience together. There was nothing we did that was sinful. When two people feel about each other the way we do, it is a blessing. I don't need some nun, priest, or bible to tell me what's good. I saw my mother and father's relationship. They were with each other twenty-four hours a day, they never tired of touching and laughing. When I saw the look in their faces when they looked at each other, their eyes sparkled, they glowed. They didn't go to church, they didn't even own a bible, yet no one, no priest, no nun, not even the pope was any better then them. They taught me to be respectful, not to take advantage of people like your Sister Caroline did to you. I was taught not to steal, not like the church who takes from poor people who struggle every week, just to feed their children, meanwhile the Pope walks around in his palace wearing fancy clothes, while hoarding millions upon millions of dollars worth of treasures in the Vatican's vaults."

Throughout his entire dissertation she did not blink an eyelash. She looked to him like a statue. He knew he had to do something to soften her fear and sorrow. "Helen, let me tell you something, you were not the only one who didn't sleep. Every night I tossed and turned in bed trying to find some reason for what happened, something that made sense to me. I struggled to figure out how something as beautiful as we had could in no time be extinguished."

Then slowly a smile appeared on Stan's face. "I lied." he paused, The impact of what he just said, and what it could mean caused her to look up, in doing so, she saw the smile on his face. "I did sleep one night. After you ran out of here I was in a daze. I went behind the bar and started drinking Irish whiskey. I'm not a big drinker, oh I like beer, but whiskey is another thing. I don't recall how many I had. I do remember my father walking in, and me trying to say hi. That's it. My father told me he had to close the bar, drag me home and throw me into my bed. He said I slept the entire day and into the next morning. When I awoke, I thought I would die. I had the biggest headache anyone ever had in the world. The room started spinning, my mouth felt like the Sahara Desert and I smelled like sewer gas. I truly wanted to die"

Relaxing a little, Helen put her hand to her mouth to stifle a chuckle. "You poor, poor man, I'm sooo sorry." Sounding like the old Helen, he put on a big hurt look and said, "It doesn't sound to me that you are at all sympathetic. I was in pain, suffering, throwing up! Could you show me a little more caring? After all, you were the cause of it."

Now, having lost any fear she had of their relationship being over, she responded," Caring yes, sympathy no.

You know my family. They are in here constantly. They want only to have a good time, and they are basically good people. I love them dearly, but you only see one side of them. I live in a house where my father comes home a little tipsy from work on a daily basis, where my brothers stink from the brewery they work at and from the beer they consume. And on weekends, do you think you are the only one that has to clean up? In a night of frolicking, right here in MacKeon's, my mother and father stumble home and can barely make it up the stairs. More than half in the bag. I mean the entire bag. Then my brothers, the dear soul's leave their marks on the toilet, in the toilet and on the floor of the bathroom; it's so bad that if I didn't clean it I would get sick. So like I said, sympathy no, it was her turn to pause, but caring… yes, yes, yes, yes, yes!"

At the same moment they fell into each other's arms. Not moving a muscle, welded together in an embrace, their cheeks touching, their eyes closed, an eternity could have passed.

New York University

College of Arts and Humanities

Admissions Department.

January 15, 1963

Dear Mr. MacKeon:

It is with great pleasure I am able to inform you that the faculty within the Language and Literature Department unanimously, arrived at the decision to offer you The Ralph Waldo Emerson Scholarship in English Literature. It is a full four year scholarship that includes room and board. The scholarship is awarded to one student a year, a student who exhibits a profound talent and commitment towards the study of English Literature. The faculty made a special effort to note that your admissions statement was insightful, brilliant, knowledgeable and beautifully written. As a sidebar, at first, the faculty could not believe your age. "No one that young could have the clarity of thought, and depth of perception." Then after checking the full entrance portfolio, reading your letters of reference, and making follow-up phone calls, all doubts were gone.

Details of the scholarship along with a letter of acceptance for you to sign will be sent to you some time next week.

Congratulations, and the best of luck. Looking forward meeting you.

Lawrence Taylor

Director of Admissions

College of Arts and Humanities

MacKeon's Bar and Grill

Saturday morning - January 20, 1963 -

"Helen would you please stop crying, please stop it. I'm not leaving you, I'm going to get an education, one that will enable me to make something of myself. I didn't plan for it, I didn't initiate the process, but when something this good falls into your hands, you just can't pass it up. School wont start until September, so we will have plenty of time to be together. Then I will be in New York City, just a few hours away. I plan on coming home every month, so we will see each other often. I will miss you too, but we don't have to start missing each other for another eight months.

I am sorry I did not tell you about the scholarship, I realize I should have. I just didn't think it could possibly happen. Mrs. Doubleday, the Librarian down at *South Bend Memorial Library*, more a friend than a librarian, thinking I should do more with my life then tend bar, initiated the process. She has acted as my mentor, and we have been discussing books seemingly forever.

She is a graduate from *N.Y.U.* and upon reading the alumni newsletter one day found out about this scholarship. Without my knowledge, she took some samples of my writing down to New York for an alumni meeting. There she showed my work to one of her old teachers. He though it was pretty good, in fact very good, and agreed with Mrs. Doubleday that I had a chance for the scholarship. He offered to gather the necessary information which then he would send to her along with an application package.

Then one day when I was taking some books out of the library, she takes me aside, and tells me what she did. Then she hands me this package of papers with a check made out to *N.Y.U.* for $100.00, the application fee, and heartily recommends I apply. I have nothing to lose. If I am not accepted and don't get the scholarship I don't have to pay her back, for the whole thing was her idea. But if I do get the scholarship, she expects me to pay the money back, not immediately, but at some point. She was right, I had nothing to lose.

She has been really good to me. I didn't want to hurt her feelings especially after all the trouble she went to, so I told her okay, I would get everything together and sent it in. Again, in my wildest dreams I never thought I had a chance, even more so after discovering the scholarship is one of the most prestigious in the world. I didn't even tell my father. In fact I put it out of my mind.

Then when I got the letter last Monday, I was in shock. I didn't know what to do, so I showed the letter to my father. He read it, shook my hand and said congratulations. I said Dad, "I can't accept this, I couldn't leave you alone. There will be no one to help you. "

He said, "son, this sounds like an opportunity of a lifetime. Years ago Mrs. Doubleday told me how smart you were. I didn't know it then, but she was right. This letter is proof she was right.

And I do believe if you are as smart as all get out, and again this letter says you are, you would be wasting your life being here with me. Don't get me wrong, I love you dearly, and I love you being here, but if I was responsible for preventing you from becoming all you can be, I just couldn't handle it.

Son I don't know a lot, but I know you would be crazy to throw away an education at a fancy New York school, with them paying for everything. And furthermore let me tell you I ain't got any crazy kids. And let me tell you something else, your mother would be very proud of you, in fact, right now she *is* proud of you. I can see her face all full of smiles, biting at the bit to tell the news to the other angels.

So there is nothing more for you to think about. You'll be packing a bag, and heading for New York City come September. I am your father, and I say so. With that he grabbed me, something he didn't do very often, and hugged me with all his might."

Still crying she said, "I know it is a great opportunity, but I will miss you. And you will meet all those girls, and you'll forget about me. I don't know what I would do if that happened. These last four years have been the best years of my life. Even though we only see each other on weekends, I know you are here. I dream about us. I can't lose you, I just can't. I will do anything if you don't go away."

With that Stan reached out and took Helen by the hands. "Look at me Helen, look at me. You have nothing, nothing to worry about. I love you. I am not going there for girls, I'm going there for an education. An education that will enable us to be together, and not worry about having to make ends meet. Isn't that what you want?

She reached up and grabbed his face, and kissed him so hard his lip started bleeding.

As the days turned into weeks, and weeks into months Helen began to change. She began to wear makeup. Not much, a light colored lip-stick, and some face powder in an attempt to cover up her freckles. Then one day he noticed she was wearing some perfume. Again not a lot, just enough to be intriguing. When in an embrace she would rub her body against him ensuring in her mind that he would notice her softness. She would continue until she noticed him getting hard.

Then on a hot day in June towards the end of their Saturday session, she informed him she wasn't wearing a bra as she guided his hand under her sweater and onto her bare breast. This time the startled party was Stan.

"Helen, what are you doing?"

"I'm just enjoying the touch of the man I love. Don't you like it?"

"I thought we agreed to stop the heavy petting before we got into trouble. You don't have to do this to show me you love me. We agreed to hold off becoming more intimate until you become eighteen."

"Well that's just around the corner, and what if I changed my mind and don't want to wait?"

"Helen I love your mind, I love your body, I love touching you, and I love our weekends. Why don't we keep it as it is for as long as we can?"

MacKeon's Bar and Grill

Saturday morning - August 18, 1963

"Dad, would it be okay if Helen and I go to the movies this afternoon? There's a movie playing Helen thought I would love! It's *Breakfast at Tiffany's*, and was written by one of my favorite authors, Truman Capote. It will only be for a couple of hours, and I'll come right back after the film."

"Go, go, don't worry about it. It won't get busy until after dinner. I can handle the place. You're a good boy and a hard worker. I forget you should have some time for yourself. Go, go enjoy yourselves." Reaching into the cash register he pulled out a couple of singles, handed it over to his son, and told him to have some popcorn on him.

When reaching the corner Stan started to turn right towards Wells Street where the theatre was located, but Helen veered him left. "Why are you turning left? The theater is three blocks down on the right."

Helen had other plans on her mind. She had thought this out clearly, and had planned this for quite a while. "Hold my hand and please don't interrupt me until I'm finished. This is something I want to do, and you will make me the happiest girl alive if you just do what I ask.

Since your father is at work he won't worry about you. I told my parents we would be going to the movies this afternoon, then I might go back to the bar and hang out with you for a while. That way they wouldn't miss me. I would like to go to your house, and slowly and passionately make love. It's the perfect plan. No one would know, just the two of us. It would be as if we were married."

"Are you crazy? We can't do that. We agreed, none of that stuff, not for a while anyway. I can't, we..., it's not right. Don't you remember what Sister Caroline said? And besides that I'm not prepared. I don't have any protection."

"Don't worry, you don't need any. I just finished my period yesterday, and have not started to ovulate yet. So protection is not necessary. As to Sister Caroline, it is none of her business what two people in love do. I want us to be together. I have been dreaming about this for weeks. Don't worry about knowing what to do. I know we are both virgins, so I have been doing a lot of research, and the more research I did, the more excited I became."

Stan had long wanted to have sex with her, but after that episode two years ago, there was no way he was going to make a move. Many an evening the mere thought of Helen's beautiful body drove him to distraction. Testosterone had been running amok within his body especially since her body became curvaceous, but he had given his word, they had decided to wait, and in his mind he knew it was the right decision. Now...

Realizing that she thought this was a necessary action, that this was her way to anchor herself in his mind and soul, he tried to maintain his rationality and convince Helen this was a dangerous course of action, that this was not something two people rushed into. But while his mind said one thing his body said another.

His masturbating had become more intense and more frequent recently. The subtle scent of her perfume had been having an effect on his libido. The face powder she was using made her look older, and more vivacious. The touch of her bare breast shot electrical pulses through his body. Yet he continued to protest, but Helen knew her strategy and planning was going to pay off. Nestling up to him she began to whisper in his ear. "This is our opportunity. You know this day has been in the making for four years. This is our chance. Everything is in place. We might not have this opportunity again. We can't pass up our moment. We have both been dreaming of doing this for a long time. You know that is true. Don't be afraid, we are no longer children, and we deserve to be able to fully love one another."

Though still protesting, he found himself allowing her to lead him towards his father's home. In somewhat of a stupor, he was being torn apart by the battle that was raging between his mind and his body. As he was recently discovering, Helen was no longer a shy young adolescent, no this was a woman who was hell bent on getting what she wanted, and she wanted him. She had always pushed her point, and fought like hell to be proven right, but now when adding sexuality to her bag of tricks, she was calling all the shots, and he knew he was fighting a losing battle.

All the way to his father's house she continued to lean her body against his and whisper encouragements.

"I love you Stan. You are my hero. I've loved you from the first time I met you. When you hold my hand, touch my shoulders, hug my body and kiss my lips I feel protected from all evil or harm. The first time you touched my breast my body went into shock. That was one of the reasons I reacted the way I did. I had never felt anything like that before. I was frightened, and so I screamed. But that was then and this is now. I love your touch and can't wait for more of it."

He was not thinking clearly. Her words, more of a mantra then a message seemed to be blocking out rational thought. And before he knew it he saw himself walking up the three steps that led to the home he was born in. Mechanically he took his keys out of his pocket and open the front door. Though he seemed to have problems moving, Helen had none. She gently maneuvered the two of them into the entry foyer, then into the living room. It seemed to Stan he was seeing the room for the first time.

Things he took for granted, now were glaring at him to be noticed. He saw bits of red thread woven into the dark brown upholstery of the sofa and arm chairs that had always been there. He had been born in this house, grew up in this house, had sat on that very sofa and chairs hundreds of times, how could he have not noticed the red thread before? Then he glanced at the wooden breakfront and tables. They used to glisten when his mother was alive, as if the sun was directly shining down on them. Now they were dull. How could he have not noticed that before? Even with the curtains drawn, and the room in semi-darkness, he was seeing details of the room he had not noticed before.

"Which is your room?" Her voice brought him back to the present, and without consciously knowing what he was doing, he pointed to his room.

He stood beside his bed as she unbuttoned her white blouse and wiggled out of the sleeves, casually allowing it to fall to the floor. His eyes glued to her every movement, his throat dry as a hot day on a sandy beach, his mind saying, "Oh my God, how could this be happening?"

Watching him standing there as rigid as a rock, sensing his discomfort, she then reached behind her back, unsnapped her bra and slowly removed it from her shoulders. He could not take his eyes off of her white skin, full breasts, and pink nipples. Noticing his stare she instinctively crossed her arms over her breasts as if to protect herself. Then a smile slowly appeared on her face. She was in control now, and she liked feeling this way. All the planning, all the research, all the doubts were slowly eroding. This was right. She was right. This was her time. As if having choreographed a dance, she then unbuttoned her skirt, and with a slow shrug of her hips dispensed it down. Then after lingering for a moment, she slid her panties down below her knees, let them fall, and nonchalantly stepped out of their reach.

He stopped breathing, embarrassed over his reaction to her nakedness. She was more beautiful than he had imagined. As his eyes traveled down over the length of her body he lingered on her pubic hair. It was as red and as wild as her hair on her head.

His erection was attempting to burst through his pants as she approached him, and suggested he get undressed. With that she turned and climbed into his bed, making herself comfortable while adjusting the pillow behind her neck.

For the first time in his life, Stan was experiencing physical ineptitude. Unable to unbuckle his belt, and unbutton his trousers, he finally with a sudden burst of strength, pulled them down. Almost knocking himself to the ground, he kicked off his shoes, and stepped out of his pants and under-shorts.

Still in his shirt and socks he lay down on the bed beside her.

All the time he was struggling, she was fascinated by the extent of control she had. Though bigger, stronger, older, and more experienced then she, it was she who was directing the moment, a thought that pleased her more than she would have believed.

Lying next to her, Stan stopped breathing. Her nakedness had frozen him in time and space. Watching him with the eyes of a hawk, Helen realized nothing was going to happen unless she made it happen, and she was going to make it happen. Not only had she written the script, and was directing the action, but was also playing the lead. This was part of life, and she knew it would bring her the man she loved.

With that awareness, she took his hand in hers, and slowly, carefully began to guide it to her body. She kissed his fingers, then lowered his hand to her neck, stopping momentarily at her clavicles. Moving on down, she placed his hand on her breast, moving it rhythmically from one to the other, making sure his fingers not only outlined their shape, but felt their form. Lingering for only a moment, she took the middle three fingers of his hand and began outlining her aureole, sending a chill throughout her body. She then proceeded to gently pressed his middle finger to outline her hard nipple.

Gulping for breadth, feeling sensations he did not know he could feel, existing in a world of an unimaginable dream, he became an ardent servant, fulfilling the will of his mistress. When she recovered from the jolt she felt from his gentle massaging her nipple, she continued journeying his hand down to her stomach. No longer in need of her guidance, he slowly began investigating the curvature of her belly, and the hills and valleys of her hips. As his hand began exploring the texture of her pubic hair, she rolled him on top of her, and guided his member into her wet channel.

At first they didn't move. Helen doing everything within her power to hide the pain she was feeling from his initial penetration. He realized he was having sexual relations, not just reading, or dreaming about it, and the thought momentarily immobilized him.

Within seconds he instinctively began thrusting his hips forward, back, forward. After no more than a dozen thrusts, he suddenly exploded inside of her while making involuntary guttural, sounds.

Though he felt spent, all energy gone, her legs wrapped around him, she would not let him go. Taking his head in both her hands she kissed him on the mouth with a passion he had not experienced before.

"You are wonderful, big, and sooo strong, I can't find the words." Ignoring her own pain, she continued stroking him and whispering loving words into his ear.

"I, I, I, I'm so ashamed. I, I couldn't hold back. I lost control, and suddenly just came."

"Stan, my love, there is nothing to be ashamed of. All the books I read said that was going to happen. It happens to every man the first time. Don't worry, I'm not worried, it will only get better. And as she began to stroke him, and play with his chest hairs, he became hard again.

Round two began moments later. Only this time things were different. As he rolled on top of her, and spread her legs apart with his knees he entered her with a power he didn't know was inside of him. As he started driving into her, she began to moan, while her body began convulsing. There was no stopping him now, he had become an involuntary pumping machine. He kept going, and going and going until he exploded a second time.

As she arched her back and called his name, he could feel every muscle in his body cry out in revelry, as a calmness took possession of his body.

May 20.2007

Huntington Apartments

Arising from his chair, Stan retrieved another *Labatts Blue* from the small, but adequate refrigerator that came with the apartment. Growing up in a bar, and eating bar food had set the tone for his eating habits. Epicurean delights had no importance in his life. In fact he was never comfortable eating in fancy restaurants, or wearing a tie. Though not thinking of himself as cheap, he believed it was crazy to pay extraordinary prices for minimum food. Why, the more restaurants charged, the smaller the portion, made no sense to him. Then again, many things in the world made no sense to him. Returning to his chair he regained his repose and returned to his past.

Those first few months at *N.Y.U.* were amazing. His dorm just across Washington Square Park, east of the *School of Language and Literature* was alive with freshman students like himself who couldn't get enough of literature. Wherever and whenever he left his room a discussion, or debate could be overheard between two or more students extolling the genius of Dickens, Zola or Dumas, or vilifying Hemmingway, Shute or Fast. Within days he discovered by listening intently, their logical arguments and knowledge of the subjects were no greater than his, in fact, he knew he could more than hold his own in those encounters. Within days of his new awareness, he became an active participant in those discussions. "My God" he remembered thinking, "this is almost as good as sex." With that thought etched in his consciousness, his mind returned to the last week in August and the first week in September, prior to his departure to New York City.

Helen had become a zealot in their coming together, and he, a more than willing participant. Noting the overt nature of their touching, and realizing it was only two weeks before Stan was to leave for school, his father understood Stan's request for time away from the bar. Smiling to himself, recalling his own courtship with his beautiful wife, and seeing his young son smitten with the Maguire girl, in such a similar way, he readily agreed to give his son all the time he asked for. At the same time, he found himself thanking God his son would soon be leaving for school, for the thought of the trouble they could get into made him very uncomfortable. Little did he know the die was already cast.

(It goes without saying) When a person plays with fire, he or she will get burned.

On his first weekend home in November, Stan was rocked with news that would alter the course of his life. Helen informed him that she had missed her period, and she thought she was pregnant, more than thought, she knew it. Not only did she know it, but had determined what they had to do.

As she informed him that there was not a lot of time, his mind reactivated, and his mouth uttered the words, "nooo, you can't be, no, it's impossible, no, no…" Then regaining a semblance of his wits, asked her what she meant by not a lot of time.

In determining how to best present the news of her pregnancy, she decided the straight-forward, non emotional approach was best. After all, Stan was bright, and always preached about using sound logic in presenting a point-of-view. She would heed his advise, and knew that eventually he would be proud of her. She had played this scene, and rehearsed the words at least a dozen times until she felt confident her words and actions would have her desired effect.

So she began to explain that after missing her period, she felt her body beginning to change, constantly feeling nauseous, and having mood swings. With no one to guide her, she had confided in Sister Caroline. After all, he was not there for her, he was in New York, and she was all alone.

The good Sister, after calming Helen down, and listening to her concerns, concurred with her assessment of the situation, and after a long discussion about morality and common sense, or the lack there-of, agreed to help. Since pregnancy was a gift from God, and Helen was not promiscuous, her solution for Helen's dismay was a quick marriage and the blessing of the church.

As early as this morning, Sister Caroline had informed Helen that she had spoken to Father Kerrigan who agreed with her counsel and would start making arrangements for Helen and Stan's betrothal to occur as early as next month. Since almost everyone in the neighborhood had seen the two of them together over the course of the last few years; and teasing the older MacKeon about the "lovey-doveyness" of the book-worms in the back of the bar had become standard fare. Even though Purvis MacKeon was not a church-going man, he was a good man, and the Maguire's considered a good family, the idea of marriage seemed feasible.

If the union took place before Helen started to show, it would matter little if the baby came early. Some might count the months, but it would be of little import. With their marriage and the forth-coming baby sanctioned by the church, all would be well.

There were no recriminations. After the initial news had an opportunity to sink in, the families were supportive. Stan's father agreed to have Helen move into Stan's room, and would be responsible for her while Stan was away at college, And the Maguire clan under the circumstances, felt no remorse that Helen was leaving the house. In this manner, there would be no shame cast on the family, one less mouth to feed, and no more moody girl to cast a pall on everyone. Only Elizabeth, though she said she would miss her twin sister, was excited that she would soon be an aunt, and have her own room.

Still in shock, Stan felt he had no where to turn. The families had taken over. After meeting with Father Kerrigan, and agreeing on a donation to St. Ignacios, renovation fund, the families announced the wedding would take place three weeks hence. It would be a small church wedding with only the immediate families in attendance, then MacKeon's Bar and Grill would host an open house for the neighborhood in celebration of the union of Helen Ethel Maguire and Stanley Purvis MacKeon.

Only Mrs. Doubleday after hearing the news argued against the "solution." His whole future was in front of him. There were other ways to handle the situation. In this day and age pregnancy doesn't have to mean a quick trip to the altar. His literary gift was rare. Nothing or no one should endanger it. She pleaded with him to talk to Helen about other alternatives, if they needed money, he should not worry, she would lend it to him. After hours of listening he agreed to try. But regardless of what did or didn't happen he promised her, he would complete his education.

His attempt to reason with Helen fell on deaf ears. The medical solution he suggested brought on an ugly tirade of obscenities. After quieting down, she stated defiantly that her pregnancy was a gift from God. It was a symbol that their union was blessed by God, and meant to be. She cautioned him never to use the "a" word in her presence again. Realizing the die had been cast, Stan acquiesced, and though not happy about the circumstances became a willing participant.

May 20, 2007

Huntington Apartments

"Jesus Christ what is wrong with me? How many times do I need to beat myself up? Enough Stan, enough!" Still in his favorite chair, Stan without thinking adjusted his glasses on his soft pudgy nose, more out of habit than need, picked up his notes for this evening's speech, and began to read.

"Vice President Foxworthy, President Ellingwood, members of the Board of Trustees, Provost Bullward, faculty, staff, student body, and honored guests, thank you so much for this distinction. It is an honor I will long treasure.

Early on in my life, as far back as my high school days, and continuing through college and graduate school, I realized that as much as I loved the written word I had no ability to create meaningful prose. Yet I knew then, and it is still true today that I wanted a life surrounded by books. I have achieved that, and I am grateful to this university, my teachers and the talented authors whose work I have consumed and am still reading. Thanks to literature, every day I travel the world, dine on phantasmagorical cuisine, fall in love with heroines, admire the fabulous feats of heroes and stand in awe at the brilliance of the men and women who have written the literature I teach.

Through literature my students and I explore the historical treatment of minorities, cast a critical eye on misogamy and misogyny, delve into private lives of the rich, the wicked and the famous, attend to that which is provocative and controversial, and through this intercourse, try to understand the roots of rigidity, and inflexibility. A seat in my class mandates each student take the responsibility for his/her beliefs, beliefs which governs our philosophies. And because I am a saucy, less than ancient Irishman, I can not help but refocus on the falling in love with the heroines part, oops... sorry about that. Is it any wonder I consider myself blessed?"

I'm sure that will evoke more than a smile and a chuckle from more than a few in the audience.

"And since I have been deemed the first speaker of a long program, and I can already taste a cold brew waiting for me at the conclusion of these presentations, I will conclude my brief remarks with the beautiful, awesome, and profound words of Dr. Martin Luther King Jr., Art Buchwald and Bertram Russell. A strange grouping you say? Welcome to my classes.

"Dr. King speaking at the Riverside Church, on April 4, 1967 said: "As I have walked among the desperate, rejected, and angry young men I have told them that Molotov cocktails and rifles would not solve their problems. I have tried of offer them my deepest compassion while maintaining my conviction that social change comes most meaningfully through nonviolent action. But they asked... and rightly so... what about Vietnam? They asked if our own nation wasn't using massive doses of violence to solve its problems to bring about the changes it wanted. Their questions hit home, and I knew that I could never again raise my voice against the violence of the oppressed in the ghettos without having first spoken clearly to the greatest purveyor of violence in the world today… my own government. For the sake of those boys, for the sake of this government, for the sake of the hundreds of thousands trembling under our violence, I cannot be silent."

After discussing Dr. King's words in class, a student asked, "Professor, why are we discussing Dr. King's words in a literature class?

My answer was simple. "It is because I believe literature, regardless of category, is experiencing ideas of permanent or universal form, be it prose, or verse, be it a letter, short story, novella, novel or any other written form."

The student pondered my words for a moment, and said, "I dig it professor."

I said, "Please don't dig it, think about it."

He said, "cool man."

I gave up.

Again, I know there will be more than a ripple of laughter heard in the auditorium.

Art Buchwald, in his book "Too Soon to say Goodbye" wrote:

People like to ask me deep questions. One day my friend Morgan asked,

"Is there a class system in heaven?"

I said, "You mean rich people and poor people?"

He said, "that's right."

I replied, "It's very possible, because rich people have built all the churches, synagogues, and mosques. Poor people don't have enough money even to fill in a stained glass window."

Morgan said, "I thought as much. Rich people probably have the best hotel rooms, and the most exclusive golfing clubs."

I said, ""It could be. Poor people can always caddy for the rich people."

Morgan asked, "Is there a dress code in heaven. Will the rich people still wear Dior, Gucci and Chanel?"

I said, "Yes, because your status in heaven will be based on how beautiful you look and how much Botox you can afford. But now Morgan, this is just conjecture. There is a possibility that everyone in heaven will be wearing the same clothes from J.C. Penny and Macy's. This might tick rich people off. I am certain they have it in their minds that their way of life will continue in heaven. I'm just guessing this, but if they can't be rich in heaven, they might not want to go there.

Morgan asked, "What about automobiles? Will the rich have Cadillacs and Acuras and the poor drive around in used Chevrolets?"

"Yes, that's the way it will be, provided they have highways there, and there is no speed limit."

Morgan asked, "And private airplanes?"

The affluent demand their right."

Morgan asked, "When you get to heaven and you're poor, can you work your way up to being rich?"

I said, "Yes, that's known as the Heavenly Dream. I heard of one man who arrived as a pizza delivery guy. In one year he had

Pizza Huts all over the sky. I guess everybody wants to know if it's even possible to be rich or poor in heaven. A few years ago a golden castle in the sky went for ten million. Now you can't even touch it for twenty-five.

"What about taxes?"

I replied, "As far as I know there are no taxes. That's why they call it heaven."

"That means there are no H&R Block stores up there."

Nope. There isn't even an IRS."

That's the best thing I have heard about heaven so far."

I said," Paying taxes is hell. Morgan, I would be a fraud if I said I knew exactly what went on in heaven. I'd like to be a rich man when I go there. You can afford to go to the opera and get better tables in the restaurants. And the beauty of it all is there is no tipping. If everybody were the same, heaven would be socialist state, and you wouldn't want to belong to that, would you?"

"Before you say, "Art Buchwald in a literature class?" Allow me to suggest that in no other genre can the profound and the profane not only co-exist, but enhance meaning.

"And because I am a romantic, I will conclude my remarks by quoting Bertram Russell.

"Three passions, simple but overwhelmingly strong, have governed my life: the longing for love, the search for knowledge, and unbearable pity for the suffering of mankind.

Those passions, like great winds, have blown me hither and thither, in a wayward course, over a deep ocean of anguish, reaching to the very verge of despair.

"I have sought love, first, because it brings ecstasy- ecstasy so great that I would often have sacrificed all the rest of life for a few hours of this joy. I have sought it, next, because it relieves loneliness-that terrible loneliness in which one shivering consciousness looks over the rim of the world into the cold unfathomable lifeless abyss. I have sought it, finally, because in the union of love I have seen, in a mystic miniature, the prefiguring vision of the heaven that saints and poets have imagined. This is what I sought and thought it might seem too good for human life, this is what-at last- I have found.

"With equal passion I have sought knowledge. I have wished to understand the hearts of men. I have wished to know why the stars shine. And I have tried to apprehend the Pythagorean power by which numbers holds sway about the flux. A little of this, but not much I have achieved.

"Love and knowledge, so far as they were possible, led upwards to the heavens. But always pity brought me back to earth. Echoes of cries of pain reverberate in my heart. Children in famine, victims tortured by oppressors, helpless old people a hated burden to their sons, and the whole world of loneliness, poverty, and pain make a mockery of what human life should be. I long to alleviate the evil, but I cannot, and I too suffer.

"This has been my life. I have found it worth living, and would gladly live it again if the chance were offered me."

"Thank you!"

Short, sweet and profound. Good job Stan! Mrs. Doubleday, I thank you, without your confidence in me, your encouragement, and, yes... your love, I would not be here, so thank you, thank you, thank you.

Yes Stan, you've did it again, and I believe I deserve one more beer before showering and get dressing for the banquet this evening."

Stan never had a problem rationalizing that he had time for one more beer. So he fetched the can, opened it, and found his favorite spot on his chair, and immediately returned to his reminiscences.

⁂

The wedding, he recalled, went off without a hitch. He seemed to have resolved whatever conflict was brewing within him about his life. After all he did love her. She was a perfect match for him. They loved the same things. Their families got along, in fact, the Maguire's, as he got to know them better, even though they had no interest in academics, were fun loving folk, and welcomed him as a son-in-law.

His father welcomed Helen, as his new daughter-in-law, and thinking back to the wedding, actually seemed a bit relieved after Stan said, "I do." With Helen out of school, and living and working side-by-side with his father, everyone was happy. In fact he remembered being a bit surprised when Helen volunteered to take Stan's place at the bar while he was away at school. With Helen at his side, his father seemed more than a tad younger, and that veil of sadness that used to accompany him daily, seemed to have disappeared.

Now in the family, the Maguire clan pitched in to help at the bar. The boys took over the heavy work, lifting storing and attaching the kegs. Other than a pint here and there, they asked for no remuneration. Mrs. Maguire would relieve Helen of bar duty from 1:00 P.M. to 4:00 P.M. daily, while cautioning her daughter to get as much rest as she could.

Elizabeth, also out of school, and now working as a salesgirl at Woolworth's down on Beacon St. would meet Helen at the bar on weekend mornings, and assumed the responsibility for clean-up.

The most surprising aspect of the blending of the families was that Helen had even begun to drink a pint or two of Guinness Ale on a daily basis, and not only drink it, but savor it.

Mrs. Doubleday, even though she was not happy with Stan's decision to marry Helen was pleased to see him return to his studies. She was also pleased that Stan continued to make an effort to see her, and report to her about school each weekend he came home.

Only Stan felt some kind of premonition of impending doom. Why, he could not fathom. Everything was working out better than he could have imagined. He had earned a 4.0 grade point average in school his first semester. He was recognized by his peers and faculty as an upcoming, if not young scholar. Though his sex life in the last few months had decreased drastically, he and Helen were doing fine.

Then the axe fell!

Toward the end of Helen's sixth month of pregnancy she was informed that the baby inside of her was no longer breathing. The doctor could give no reason for the tragedy, only that it had happened. The second tragedy she was told was that for her health reasons she had to carry the dead fetus inside of her for the full term. The doctor said he would see her every two weeks for the next three months to make sure she didn't suffer any additional effects. She was healthy, and he was going to make sure she stayed that way. He then said he would perform an autopsy on the baby when she delivered, only then would he be in a position to tell her what happened and why it happened.

Helen did not remember dressing, nor what happened next.

Sister Caroline discovered her sitting in the last pew of St. Ignatius sometime around six that evening, only after receiving a frantic phone call from Mr. MacKeon. After calming him down, he explained that Helen had a doctor's appointment at 1:30 P.M. that afternoon. She was in fine spirits when she left his place of business that afternoon and he called and found out she did arrive at the doctor's office on time. He then shared with the sister the news he was told by the doctor about the terrible tragedy. Since then he, and the Maguire's have been searching far and wide for her, with no luck. Could she help?

"Mr. MacKeon? This is Sister Caroline at St Ignatius. I found Helen sitting by herself in the church. No harm has befallen her, but she seems to be in a state of shock, unable to say much of anything. She is now with me in my study. Please inform the Maguire family that no harm has befallen her, and she is with me. They know of our relationship.

I will personally escort her home when she is up to it, and able to navigate the streets. Please don't worry, I will take good care of her. I have known her for most of her life, and I believe she needs someone like me to talk with right now. I will call you at your establishment when we are ready to leave the church.

You prefer to pick her up here. I understand. I will call you when I believe she is ready to go home, and you can come and get her. No, thank you is not necessary. Each of us does the work God has set us up to do. Yes, I will call. Now good bye."

Stan was not informed of what had happened until he arrived in Boston late Friday evening. Arriving at the bus depot around 9:00 P.M., he decided the 16 block walk from the depot to his father's bar would do him good. It had been a rough week, and the fresh air would feel wonderful.

He was almost finished with the paper on Carl Sandburg, and was looking forward to the opportunity of discussing his work with Mrs. Doubleday. He felt this was his best work so far, and he really wanted to share it with her.

Before he even entered MacKeon's he knew something was amiss. Usually by 9:30 P.M. on a Friday evening the noise level from MacKeon's could be heard a block and a half away. All he heard tonight from outside the bar was a low buzz. A cold fire shot through his body as he entered the bar. The usuals were there, but the joy and the laughter was missing. Adding to his confusion he saw his father-in-law behind the bar, not his father. In fact, his father was no where in sight.

Upon seeing him enter, Elizabeth ran up to him, and hugged him tight saying, "I'm sorry, I'm so sorry." At the same time, Mrs. Maguire came to him, took him by the hand and guided him to a table.

"Sit down my son, I have some bad news."

"What, what is it? Is my father okay? Helen, where is she, is she okay?"

"Helen is okay, and your father is fine. In fact he should be here any moment with Helen. Your father went to pick her up from Sister Caroline's.

She lost the baby today."

"What?"

"The baby is dead. The doctor doesn't know why the baby died. He just knows it did, and Helen is in a state of shock."

"When, where, how…?"

"We don't know, we will find out, but right now we just don't know."

May 20, 2007

Huntington Apartments

Knowing he dare not drink another beer without something in his stomach, or he was apt to make a total fool of himself at the banquet tonight, he simply sat in his chair, not moving just recalling that moment when his life had changed.

Something in Helen had snapped. He had become the source of all her woes. It was his fault the baby died. God had punished her for marrying a Godless man. He had ruined her life. After all, she was a good Catholic; she went to church and confession every week. Not him. He railed at God. He was disparaging to the church. It was obvious to her that God didn't want any part of him in a child of God, and because she had married him, she was being punished.

It was his fault she started drinking, and she knew that was probably the reason the baby had died. It was his beer, coming from his bar, paid for with his money. Evil, evil. She would never set foot in that evil place again. All those sinners, all doing the devil's work.

It didn't matter what anyone said, she knew the truth. Sister Caroline tried. Father Kerrigan tried. Her mother tried. Her sister tried. No, she knew the truth. They were trying to make her feel better. No, she knew the truth. God was punishing her for her husband's evil.

When Stan tried touching her, she pushed him away. "Don't ever touch me again! You are evil incarnate. Don't come near me. If you do I will scream." Though she was cordial to Stan's father, the only time she spoke to Stan was to make a derisive remark. Even though they lived in the same house; slept in the same bed, they were strangers.

She stopped coming to work at MacKeon's, wanted nothing to do with her family, and started attending church every day. When she wasn't in church she sat around Stan's father's house nibbling on junk food, reading passages from the bible, or simply mumbling. She began to put on weight, and it seemed with each pound she put on, the more remote she became.

A year and a half had passed, and Helen had become almost a recluse. She spent more and more time at church, but even stopped acknowledging Sister Caroline. No one could reach her, and she reached out for no one.

Stan, at this point made, it home once every six weeks, if that.

Then one evening Father Kerrigan called Mr. MacKeon and asked him to set up a meeting with Stan, himself, and the Maguire's. Father Kerrigan said the situation with Helen had become dire. He was afraid she might hurt herself, or others if something wasn't done soon. He had observed her becoming angrier and angrier, totally oblivious to anything and anyone around her, and having loud conversations with herself.

Since he knew of the situation with Stan being away at college; Mr. MacKeon, with no one to help at the bar and at the same time, providing for Helen at home; with the Maguire's struggling to pay the bills and broken hearted by their daughter's circumstances, he had taken it upon himself to do some research.

Through a contact at Catholic Services, he had located a Catholic live-in facility approximately 50 miles northeast of Boston that served people with mild to severe mental trauma. There she could get professional help, and hopefully within time be able to re-join her loved ones. He had also checked with social services, and they assured him based on what he said, that they would be able to pick up the cost of her being a in-patient at that facility.

The meeting was held, and all present were in agreement that Father Kerrigan's suggestion was in the best interest of Helen and everyone else. Arrangements were made, and two weeks later Mr. MacKeon, and Sister Caroline, the only people Helen would let near her, rented a car and drove her to her new home.

Stan was informed that if he truly wanted one, he could petition the Holy Father in Rome for an annulment. Father Kerrigan and Sister Caroline would help him through the complicated process and support his position.

Stan was grateful for their offer, but after some consideration, declined. His life would be academia. He didn't want, or feel, he needed children of his own. Marriage was a covenant he wanted nothing to do with. And who knows, if it is in the cards, someday Helen might revert back to being the beautiful, effervescent young spirit he had fallen in love with.

May 20, 2007

Huntington Apartments

"Yeah, that was a long time ago, seemingly life-times ago."

Thinking about Helen, his past and the unpredictable path that had led him to where he was now was something Stan did not do often. At least he tried not to do too often. Usually he was successful. Well, that is not entirely true. Anytime he saw a young woman with red hair, he thought about Helen. Anytime he saw a tall young lady, or a freckled young lady, or a sparkle of adventure in a young woman's eyes he thought of Helen. Like it or not, she was etched into his memory banks permanently. Though he had a number of liaisons with a number of different women over the years, he could not stop himself from comparing them to Helen, and in doing so, each and everyone of them paled by comparison.

Though quick to admit his married life was nothing to write home about, the years before were wonderful. She was really his first student, and the Outstanding Teacher's Award he received today should be shared with her.

Then without warning or his eyes welled up with tears.

"Fuck it! One more beer can't hurt."

After drying his eyes, he struggled out of his chair, and got another beer. Pulling the tab on the can, he lifted his beer into the air and began reciting of one of his favorite pieces of prose he had discovered in a book of essays, entitled *Mindscapes*, by an obscure author named Jack Slutzky.

"Love is the knowledge that imperfection is necessary to experience perfection. That honest relationships birth substance. That to withstand the test of time all four seasons must have the opportunity to input their own kind of truth. That the logic of nature in its infinite wisdom may be the only guarantee of tomorrow.

Isn't it nice to know that if the frozen ground of Winter is here… the thaw of Spring, and the bloom of Summer is closer than the just fallen leaves of Fall.

That balance, contrast, and lots of hard work pay off in the substance of life, and/or the quality of love.

When two make one greater than its sum… when one becomes stronger and more independent because it is part of two.

Love is poetry, and painting, and literature, oh yes, literature, and rockets, and hearts and flowers, and cupids, and electric blankets, and open windows seductively allowing in the fragrance of the morning air.

Love is the balance of all things.

But like the petals of the rose do not the flower make… love can not be measured in memories of what was, or what will be, but in the desire to continue experiencing, growing, laughing, crying and always, always affording your other the right to be all of her/himself."

"Helen, here's to you, and to me and for what we were, and hopefully for what we will be again.

Skoal!"

With that he downed the entire can of beer in slightly more than one swallow. "Stanley Purvis MacKeon, you are truly a romantic, I salute you. And now to the shower, the banquet, and who knows what tomorrow."

Over the sound of the shower, in a crackly baritone voice, *Danny Boy* could be heard.

Book Two
Earl Starkvisor

May 20, 2007

8540 Don Quixote Drive(an elegant 2,400 sq. ft. patio home, in a gated community 3 ½ miles southeast of cam us)

Standing in front of a huge bay window in his study, looking down on an equally large pond which had been adopted by two magnificent blue herons elegantly standing on a log which somehow had found itself in the pond, Earl said to himself, "I did it again." Turning to face the wall across from where he was standing, behind a gleaming stainless steel and glass bar accompanied by six matching stainless steel and acrylic stools, Earl scanned the large array of plaques, degrees, awards and citations he had amassed over the years and said out loud, "Not bad for a size deprived, not so good-looking, prematurely bald kid from an inner-city neighborhood, raised by a single mother who barely eked out a living. Not bad indeed!"

Finding a spot for his newest award might be somewhat difficult. He would definitely have to move things around he thought, but not now. Now was the time for the first of two martinis he afforded himself daily.

Walking behind the bar he reached down to the small refrigerator located under the bar, opened the door and removed a bottle of *Zeer Oude Genever*, special Dutch gin he loved, along with a bottle of martini rocks (porous small rocks the size of olives in a jar of vermouth), and a chilled glass, one of a set of twelve he was given by *Corning Glass* for his contributions in the development of a new line of ceramic conductors.

As deftly as a surgeon performing a complex operation, he removed one of the rocks from the jar, and carefully placed it in his glass, knowing it would exude the perfect amount of vermouth to produce the perfect martini. Earl was a stickler for proportions and perfection.

After returning the elements of this enjoyable endeavor to exactly the right place, he lifted his glass and said to no one in particular, "Here's to Mom, without you none of this would have been possible. I love you."

April 25, 1947

Brooklyn, New York

Earl Starkvisor could be accused of being short, but no one in his or her right mind would put themselves between him and a goal he was pursuing. From his earliest memory, if he wanted something, he got it. In fact, his mother was fond of telling the story that when he was first born the doctor did what every delivering doctor did in those days, hold him upside down by his two feet, and smack him on the backside. Earl's response, even though he weighed less than five pounds, was so powerful and angry that he scared the doctor into almost dropping him. Looking sympathetically at the mother the doctor said, "Mrs. Starkvisor, he might be small, but I guarantee you, he will be a hand-full."

It was not an easy birth, complications set in, and Margerie Starkvisor was told that Earl was to be her only child. Once the shock wore off, the pragmatism she got from her father, and the iron will she got from her mother was activated. She vowed at that moment, to be the best mother she could be to her only child.

He was not an attractive child. His nose a little big, his eyes a little small, and the rest of him skin and bones, but to his mother, he was sheer beauty. Her cronies, not kind, made comments. For every, "Wow, look at that baby, interesting looking, isn't he?"

She, cuddling her son would say, "Earl, Earl, my son, you are so beautiful, so wonderful, I love you so."

For every, "Margerie, where's the rest of him, ha ha, this took you nine months?"

She would respond, "don't listen to those idiots, you are everything I wanted, and I can tell from your eyes, you are very bright."

A child of Earl's stature could not have had a better mother than Margerie Starkvisor. She might have given birth to a small child, but she would make sure he would be big in life. From day one, she read to him, talked to him, sang to him, played games with him, and caressed him. Never once did she raise her voice to him in anger, nor punish him. Her mothering methodology was demonstration, and discussion. Nothing was wrong or bad. It might not yet be as right as it could be, and would be; not yet as good as it should be, and will be.

Not having any money, his mother was constantly creating cut-out shaped numbers from different weight cardboards she found in the house or around the building they lived, then colored them with bright colors. Wherever she went she searched out simple elements of different textures to add to Earl's toy box. When she wasn't engaged in some household duty, she was demonstrating creative processes of putting shapes and elements together. That's why Earl had no problem being alone, for there was always something to do with all the toys his mother had given him. And with the knowledge that his mother was near, he never allowed fear to enter his being. Even as a grown-up, Earl could smell his mother's essence, touch his mother's warm skin, and hear her gentle melodic voice.

Earl didn't see much of his father. Like most fathers in those days, he found work where ever he could and would work seven days a week, if he could. When the opportunity to work more hours was offered to him, he would work until he dropped, which he did at the age of thirty-eight. When his heart stopped.

By the time Earl was in the first grade, he was reading on a fifth grade level. Even more astounding was the fact that he loved numbers, and was proficient in multiplication, division, addition and subtraction. Even more astounding was his ability to make others around him feel comfortable. When he wasn't reading, he was playing with numbers. When he wasn't playing with numbers, he was politicking. Three skills that would define his life.

By the third grade every teacher, and administrator in the school had heard of Earl Starkvisor, the child prodigy. His capacity for learning was mind-boggling. The charm he exuded was captivating, and for an eight year old, his attitude and outlook on life refreshing.

You would think others would be jealous of him. That just wasn't the case. His capacity for making others feel comfortable around him was as staggering as his prodigious capacity for learning. Not that others wanted to be his friend, no, that wasn't the case, others accepted him with a benign, and gentle respect. Earl had no problem with that, he wanted for nothing, and other than his mother, needed no one.

By the sixth grade he had completed his high school education. He got a 98 on his English Regents exam, 100 on Geometry, Algebra, Trigonometry, Calculus and Solar Geometry Regents exams. A 97 on Physics Regent exam *(3 points were deducted when he omitted the word "millimeter". Since the question pertained to millimeters, he assumed it was a given).* He also got a 99 on his Chemistry, Biology and Earth Science Regents exams. American History, World History he aced as well.

Having completed his high school education in the sixth grade at eleven years of age, and having compulsory education in this country till the age of eighteen, the school board was going crazy trying to figure out what to do with him.

This was when the *New York Sunday Times, Magazine Section* decided to feature the child wonder in their magazine. With national exposure the school board began to receive inquiries about Earl. Soon Earl and his mother were being interviewed by representatives of a horde of schools and universities.

Three days before the close of the school year, after reviewing a variety of offers from a variety of sources, with the kind assistance of the school principal, and an interested member of the school board, who just happened to be an engineer, the decision was made for Earl to become a student at the *Massachusetts Institute of Technology, M.I.T.* They not only offered Earl a full scholarship, special housing on the university plus all expenses for him and his mother to move to Cambridge. Many universities had offered basically the same, what separated *M.I.T.'s* offer from the others was the inclusion of a full-time mentor.

At precisely 3:20, the exact moment their appointment was set for, April O'Connor knocked on the door of the Starkvisor apartment. She was politely ushered in, and made to feel welcome. There she presented *M.I.T.'s* offer speaking directly to Earl and his mother, not at them as so many people recently had done.

Right off the bat, Earl and his mother liked this lady. She was a woman in her mid-thirties. She stood 5'5" tall, weighed in at 131 pounds, had dark brown wavy hair down to her shoulders, wore a conservative light-brown linen skirt, with a blue blazer, a white blouse offset with a large amber pin and amber ear-rings. Glancing at each other, the Starkvisor's sensed the woman across from them was as affable as she was confident and precise.

April O'Connor explained that she had just graduated from *M.I.T.'s* School of Engineering, having majored in Aeronautics and Astronautics.

Though offered a number of positions, she felt she was not ready to enter the work-place. She just believed she needed some time to allow the knowledge she had acquired to transfer over into applied knowledge. When the university offered her this opportunity, she decided it would be perfect. If the Starkvisor's accepted *M.I.T.'s* offer, she had agreed to be Earl's mentor for the full academic year. That meant the university would arrange for her to live in an apartment next to the Starkvisor's. Being in such close proximity, it would be easy for her to aid and assist Mrs. Starkvisor in acclimating to her new environment, and adjusting to new living conditions, but her first priory would be Earl. To that end, she would accompany young Earl to his classes, take notes, tutor and do anything necessary to insure his success.

April and Margerie hit it off immediately.

April O'Connor

Having recently graduated with high honors, April O'Connor was tired. Having struggled for the last four years to be accepted as an equal, she did not feel ready to continue struggling in a predominately male arena. When *M.I.T.* offered her this opportunity to possibly mentor the Starkvisor's, she jumped on it. If it didn't work out, she was sure something else would. Granted the money was not as good as she was qualified to earn on the open market, but if it did work out, a year's employment was guaranteed; her apartment would be paid for; her stipend acceptable, and the year she assumed, would grant her the time and the opportunity to re-energize herself.

Living on her own since the age of eighteen, when both her parents were killed by a drunk driver, April by necessity had developed powerful coping skills. With her older brother Charles, living in Vancouver, Canada for the last six years with his partner, and her older sister a divorced mother of two down in Sarasota, Florida, April knew she was on her own.

Once her parent's estate had been settled, and the wrongful death money she was awarded by the insurance company deposited in the bank, April decided to begin her education by traveling. Her father, an automobile engineer had always driven, and self-maintained a Volvo, and at his side she had learned the art of automotive maintenance. So her first order of business was to purchase a second-hand Volvo sedan, fill up the trunk with her father's tools, and use the back seats for her personal possessions. With that accomplished, she began her pilgrimage across the country.

Twelve years, and forty-four states later, April made it back to Boston hungry to do something more with her life, and tired of being a vagabond. After some initial research, she applied to *M.I.T.*, was accepted, and began her formal education.

She loved learning as her transcript bore out, but taking shit from most of her male teachers and co-students wore her out. Being older, more mature, and goal oriented than most of the students, after a time, they simply ignored her, and that was fine with April. It was the male chauvinist faculty who pulled her strings, and drove her at times to drink.

With April O'Connor's help the Starkvisor's were all settled in to their new residences by July 10th, and by the start of the new school year were fully familiar with *M.I.T.*, Cambridge, Massachusetts and beginning to enjoy the wonders of Boston. One of Earl's fondest memories of that time was sitting between his mother, and April in awe of the quality of the sound emanating from *the Hatch Memorial Shell* along side the Charles River. As he got older, his taste in music moved from the pop scene to Mozart, Bach and Stravinsky. Nevertheless every time he heard a recording of Arthur Fiedler, and the Boston Pops he immediately became a young boy again seated between his two favorite women.

April was outside his door every morning waiting to escort him to class. The strange looking couple was initially greeted even more strangely when entering a new class. In preparation for their arrival, each professor had been given notice and a background folio about Earl. And each chose to introduce Earl, and his note-taker to the class on the first day. After the first week, students began to realize this was not a stunt. Earl was a serious student, and intellectually equal to them. Within a short time, the novelty of having a child prodigy in their class faded away.

As he had done all his life, it didn't take long for Earl, only now with April's help to win the minds and some of the hearts of his classmates, teachers, staff persons.

Within the first month of the semester April was invited by Earl's mother to take her meals with them. Since she couldn't think of a single reason not to accept the generous offer, she gratefully said yes, and dinners and weekend meals became a chatty dining experience. Earl had become like her little brother, and Margerie, a great friend. The prodigy, the pragmatist, and the optimist; a combination that made every day bright, joyful and fulfilling.

When Earl retired for evening with the knowledge he was loved by two woman, Margerie and April would sit in the kitchen and talk and talk until past eleven. This enterprise of three special people, needing each other and caring for each other worked out better than anyone could have conceived.

As the academic year was nearing it's end, April began weaning Earl off the amount of support she had been providing him. She taught him a shorthand which would enable him to take his own notes. Their tutoring sessions evolved into discussions of the viability and applicability of the material. As Earl was proving himself highly capable of handling himself in the classroom and laboratory, April began to merely escort Earl to the targeted academic building, then assured him she would be there at lunch-time with the wonderful meal Margerie prepared, then leave him. After a few days of trepidation, he began to enjoy the independence, although the knowledge April would be there to escort him home when classes ended for the day was comforting.

Her strategy worked well, and Earl began to depend on her less and less. With more free time on her hands, April began to spend more time with Margerie. The two of them loved each others company, and soon became comfortable enough with the other, to begin sharing each one's personal history.

As the year came to an end, April was notified her contract would not be renewed. She had done a fine job. The university was grateful for her diligence, and her professionalism, and would write a letter of recommendation at her request.

The notification jolted her out of her dream-like state that one day would surely follow another. An emotional ennui took-up residence within her being. What would she do? She had learned to love Earl more than she did her own brother. Margerie had become her best friend. Every day in the past year they had talked, shared feelings, shared a warm touch on the arm, a gentle pat on the back, or a simple caress.

Once aware of the situation, Margerie and Earl agreed something had to be done. They didn't want to lose her. Margerie suggested and Earl readily agreed to ask April to move in with them, and since Margerie's room was large, equipped with a queen size bed, there would be ample room for the two of them. Earl thought it was a perfect solution enabling the three of them to remain together.

The next evening, sitting down at dinner, Margerie, at Earl's urging, shared the plan the Starkvisor's had come up with. Explaining they felt April was more family than friend, and without her friendship, guidance and worldliness they would feel all alone and lost in an intimidating environment.

Having spent most of the last eighteen years of her life predominantly on her own, this year felt blissful, but not having her own space… she wasn't sure. Not wanting to take no for an answer, Margerie and Earl began to overwhelm her with loving comments and tenderness. Slowly she accepted the realization that the past was the past, and if one was to survive in this world, one would need to grasp opportunity when it came knocking. She truly loved the Starkvisor's. If she accepted their offer, she would never have to feel alone again. Sharing a bedroom with Margerie would not be a problem. She didn't possess a lot of personal things, and as she realized she had never been closer to another human being than Margerie.

She agreed.

Living next door to each other, the entire move entailed transporting four small suitcases (housing her entire wardrobe and all her possessions) about sixty feet. A small dresser would be all she needed to accommodate everything she owned.

The university also agreed to let her keep her parking spot, if she agreed to register for one class in pursuit of a master's degree. And since April was in essence the Starkvisor's personal guide (knowing her presence was a major factor in the Starkvisor's successful acclimation) and chauffer, it sounded like a good deal all around.

Over the years, April had been very wise financially. She wisely invested the settlement money she received from her parents wrongful death claim from the insurance company, in "blue chip" stocks, plus a couple of "start-up" companies. A pleasant surprise was when two of the start-up stocks split three for one, and five for one. Not being much of a gambler, within the year she cashed those stocks in for guaranteed T notes. All and all, she had accrued a rather substantial investment portfolio, including a decent annuity which supplied her with most of the funds she needed to live on, so the loss of the stipend the university paid her was not a problem. Nevertheless she decided a part-time job would be in everyone's best interest.

In that manner she would have a little extra money to spend, and give her and Margerie some time apart, allowing each private time and space. April moved in and felt right at home. Life could not have been better for the Starkvisor's and O'Connor.

By Earl's senior year the number of articles and features about *M.I.T.'s* prodigy slowed down to about one a month, yet the university had no concerns. The publicity the university had received from the linkage of Earl Starkvisor to *M.I.T.* had translated into endowment money, and increased student enrollment. The four years Earl was a student there exceeded the wildest dreams of the Director of Administrative Staff Orientation and Resources, the man who first suggested they offer a scholarship to Earl. The General Endowment Fund had increased by 40%, and even though student enrollment had recently peaked, the quality of the applicants rose.

Earl loved being at *M.I.T.*, and *M.I.T.* loved having Earl as a student. Not only was he a dazzling, effervescent student with a mind rarely seen, but he had a special gift for knowing what to say at the right time. He might have looked fifteen, but he had an emotional maturity of an experienced adult.

Having accomplished something rarely seen, a 4.0 grade point average, acing every class he took, *M.I.T.* was pleased to find out that Earl wanted to continue his studies there.

He intuitively knew he needed to develop management skills, for he realized his potential to achieve greatness. To achieve that he would need to have the skills to manage people and processes. The *Joint Engineering and Management Graduate Program* was a perfect fit for his plan. The *College of Engineering* was thrilled.

With the future in place, Earl had devised a plan for himself, a personal time-line. He would stay in Cambridge three more years, push himself to accomplish everything he could academically, including if possible, two master's degrees. Then at the age of eighteen he would strike out on his own and go elsewhere to pursue a doctorate's degree.

As he got older, the two women he so cared about, loved him so much he was beginning to feel smothered. When he started looking into graduate programs he had shared with his mother and April that *Stanford* was really interested in him. It made him feel good enough to write and ask about scholarship money.

"Well, Mom, April what do you think?" He was not prepared for their reaction… which was nothing, absolutely nothing.

They simply sat at the kitchen table wide-eyed, as if frozen in space. They had not been prepared, nor even thought about Earl going off somewhere. Suddenly the reality of their future was right before their eyes. Earl was not a child anymore. He was fifteen, with the inquisitive mind of a fifteen year old, and had the desires of a fifteen year old. They realized their perfect triad was no longer impervious to time.

Sensing their discomfort, Earl engineered the conversation back to *M.I.T.*, stating that even though Stanford intrigued him, he was still favoring *M.I.T.'s Joint Engineering and Management Graduate Program.* He had planned to write to *Stanford* to merely broaden his knowledge about universities on the west coast. The moment he uttered those words, he saw relief reappear on their faces. It was shortly after this conversation that his plan for the future was solidified.

In many states, eighteen was the age when a teen-ager became an adult, or at least, a quasi-adult. Thus eighteen would become the age of his independence. He rationalized that in his case patience was more than a virtue, and two years would afford him the opportunity to gently and lovingly wean him from his two loving ladies.

Over the course of the last four years, his mother and April had become more than just friends. How or when that exactly happened he wasn't sure, but he knew beyond a shadow of doubt it had. There was no dialogue about it, nor any overt behavior. Nevertheless, it was obvious to Earl. He had observed them when they didn't know he was watching; hand holding, nestling together on the sofa, subtle looks and warm secret smiles. Earl was not unhappy with the development. He thought, what could be better than having the two women he loved, love each other? Not only that, but when time came for him to go out on his own, they would have each other.

Since all three of them had always communicated honestly with each other, he was a little dismayed as to why they were uncomfortable discussing their deepening relationship with him. Each time he tried to speak to the topic, their body language showed their discomfort. After a few aborted attempts, he realized this was not the time for persistence. Maybe he thought he was too young to understand.

Over the course of the last two years, Earl was going through a number of changes. He was still the proverbial "110 lb. weakling", but now he had begun dreaming of, and noticing the few coeds in his classes. He had started to develop pubic hair, and hair under his arms. And though a quick look in the mirror told him he was not ready to begin shaving, he knew the time was not far into the future. With these changes occurring, he had attempted a number of times to engage his mother in a discussion of what was happening to him. The minute he brought it up, was the minute his mother would change the subject.

He and his mother, and in the last two years, April, had no secrets, or so he thought. Now each time he broached the subject his mother's face would turn pinkish-red, and she would discover something she needed to do immediately. April taking his mother's lead would depart for premises unknown. He was becoming a frustrated young man.

In his *Aeronautical Systems Laboratory* class he made friends with the only two female students in the class, Gert Thomkins and Davida Kirsch. They became so friendly that each had a t-shirt made with the letters TW&AP (two women and a prodigy) printed on the front. Since the three of them felt nothing in common with the rest of the class, intrinsically knowing they were smarter than the other students in the class, they formed their own little society.

At lunchtime one afternoon while sitting at a picnic table just behind the Engineering building, the two women couldn't help but notice Earl was not his usual effervescent self. After inquiring a number of times what the problem was, and getting no response they decided it was probably time to leave. Seeing his two friends getting ready to depart, his panic overcame his shyness, and he blurted out a plea for help.

"Please don't go. I, I need to talk. Things are happening to me, and I am not comfortable. I tried talking to my mother and April, but both find things to do the moment I start the conversation. One time I inadvertently mentioned the word, "sex." They both turned beet red, and left the apartment. I'm left with feelings I can't talk about, desires I don't understand. I'm having trouble concentrating on anything but what is happening to me."

Other than being much older than Earl, he was fun to be with, and with him to depend on academically, they were breezing through their classes. He was utterly fascinating, and in spite of the age difference, they really had taken a liking to him. The male chauvinism they felt all around them was not any part of Earl's being; his mind a wonder beyond belief, his charm totally engaging. Remembering their own adolescence, how could they not take this 110 pound man-child under their wings?

As he detailed his problems, they gave each other a knowing look and tried to explain to Earl that the problem was not his mother, nor April. In fact the problem was not even a problem. He was leaving his childhood, and was on the verge of entering manhood. It was clear to them his mother was not prepared for this turn of events, as many mothers weren't. Sons usually talk to their fathers, or brothers, or male friends.

As they assuaged his fears about feeling lost, humanized the biology of his body, and calmed his fear of being small. They volunteered themselves to be his surrogate, sexual advisors. They would help him enter manhood.

Over the course of the next two years knowledge replaced fear and confusion and Earl became comfortable with his sexuality. He was coming to terms with who he was and what he was, and with Gert and Davida's able assistance his manliness would never again come into question. Never once did his mother, and/or April inquire about the amount of time he was now spending away from the apartment. Inwardly his mother was saddened knowing her child was no longer her baby, nor was he hers alone. Those magic moments holding him to her breast, sensing the miracle he was; the game playing and the laughter they shared was to be no more. Yet outwardly she was pleased, seeing him grow into the person he would become, and content, as long as he didn't try to renew his questions about his, or her sexuality.

Since there could never be overt lies between them, certain questions were not asked, and terms such as, "learning groups," and "study groups" became descriptors of his activities. A tacit understanding between the members of the household was developed, and no one questioned him about his activities away from the apartment.

True to his word, two months after reaching his eighteenth birthday, on graduation day Earl Starkvisor achieved the distinction of *Outstanding Scholar*, and was awarded a master's degree in both *Engineering and Management Studies*, and in *Brain and Cognitive Science.*

At the completion of commencement services, after disposing of his cap, gown and cape, basking in the feeling of accomplishment, he took a few moments to contemplate this moment in time and space. He knew this would signal-in the end of book two of his life, and usher in the beginning of book three. A feeling of sadness and gladness permeated his body. "Yes," he thought, it was frightening to think he would soon be leaving his safe-nest, his haven… to pursue his destiny, and he would be doing it on his own. But at the same time he knew his Mom and

April would be with him in spirit wherever fate had determined he was to go.

They would be fine. They had already found an apartment in Boston in a recently converted brownstone, and were preparing to move in on the following Wednesday. The next day he would board a train which would take him to the west coast. Life was good, life was very good!

Arrangements had been made to meet his Mom and April beside the quad at precisely twelve noon. Since lateness was one of those things he was not comfortable with, he pushed his way through the horde of graduates, saying "excuse me" all the time. Once outside the building broke into a slow run. At the split-second he arrived from the north, his Mom and April arrived from the east, and Davida and Gert arrived from the west.

Unaware that Davida and Gert were on a bee-line towards him he rushed into his mother's and April's arms amid shouts of joy and screams of happiness. In no more than a second, the threesome became a five-some as Davida and Gert joined the party. Everybody was hugging and kissing with only Earl knowing who each person was.

"Mom, April, I'd like you to meet two dear friends of mine, Gert Thomkins and Davida Kirsch. Starting to blush, something he never did, he continued, "they are member's of my study group, and without their help, I don't know what I would have done."

"We have heard all about you Mrs. Starkvisor and Ms. O'Connor, April as Earl calls you. It is a pleasure to finally meet you. Earl is a special young man. It is not often a person of his intelligence is matched with an equal amount of goodness. We know he will accomplish great things in his lifetime, and the little we were able to do for him, was nothing compared to the help he has been for us. He is just one special human being. We will take a part of Earl within our hearts where ever we go."

Turning their attention to Earl, Gert began, "Earl, we have to be going, have a train to catch, we just wanted the opportunity to wish you the best. It was a joy being with you for these few years. Knock 'em dead out west, and remember size never was nor will be an issue. It is what you do with what you have, that is important." With that departing statement, Davida, then Gert planted a big kiss right on his mouth. "Bye" they said.

Before Earl's mother or April had a chance to say a word they rushed off into the crowd. Looking back at Earl standing there with a sheepish grin on his face, the two women looked at each other, nodded their heads, broke into a smile and resumed hugging their little man-child"

May 20, 2007

8540 Don Quixote Drive

Sipping his extra, extra dry martini, Earl's mind traveled back to his graduation day in 1962, his *Independence Day*. He had waited three years for that time to come. Though he dearly loved his Mom and April, he knew it was time to go. They had matured into a committed couple, complete in their togetherness. His absence would merely allow them to focus all their energies on each other, without worrying about him. He knew they would miss him, as he them, but after a time they would come to terms with his venturing forth in the world on his own.

He started to chuckle as he recalled the farewell scene at the quad after the graduation ceremonies had been completed. It was for the first and only time his mother and April encountered Gert and Davida. He had lost track of those two women in the last ten years. In fact, the last time he spoke with Gert she mentioned she had not spoken with Davida for a number of years.

Gert, now into her third marriage, had four children, two from her first and one each from numbers two and three. Davida when last heard of, had emigrated to Israel and become an officer in the Haganah, the Israeli army.

They were terrific women Earl reminisced. Without their help he would have gone crazy. Their gentility, guidance and caring allowed him to come to terms with himself. They taught him that giving was as good as receiving. That love and lovemaking comes in various forms, none better than the other, just different, and that in a mutual, honest relationship, nothing is "evil" or "dirty."

While thinking of Davida and Gert, he couldn't help but think of his one great love, Ellen. She could have been the one. Yes, how life could have been different if…

Sipping an empty glass brought him out of his revelry. "Well Earl, since you do know how to make a great martini, and in homage to your talent, and to Ellen, Ellen Renee Somers, I think you deserve to have another.

Stanford University turned out to be everything and more than Earl had dreamt of. It's 8,200 acre campus located in the heart of Silicone Valley, between San Francisco and San Jose was paradise. The flora totally different than back East, the weather, balmy and bright was close to Earl's idea of perfection.

With layovers, transfers, and the inconveniences of traveling by rail, his journey out west took four days, and ended when he de-boarded the train at Palm Drive in downtown Palo Alto. A little shaky and a little frightened, considering these had been the first four days he had ever been alone, with no mother, no Alice, no professors to look out for him, it was now up to him to bring to fruition his dreams.

And he would!

Never having doubted his ability, nor his decision to go west, he took a deep breath, threw his shoulders back in an effort to make himself feel taller, and marched forward into the rest of his life.

Armed with the knowledge that *"Marguerite"* the *Stanford* shuttle bus offered continuous service to campus till 7:30 pm, he chose to stroll around downtown to begin to familiarize himself with the outskirts of what would be his new home.

The Palm Drive Train Depot, of Palo Alto was located two blocks east of Main Street, the town's main drag. Earl marveled at the number of stores in town catering to students. thoroughly enjoying himself, being alone in a city for the first time in his life, he began taking note and made a mental map of the stores he would visit in the future.

Here was a community that obviously depended on the student population to exist, ergo catered to college students needs, and he now saw himself as a student the stores would be catering to. It felt good, and in a sad, but glad way, he knew his earlier life with his mom and Alice would never be again. He knew he could never live home again, for he now thought himself a person of the world.

Initially he thought Palo Alto was like a miniature Cambridge, but more spread out, and simply abounding with the flora of the west coast. But as he continued his journey through, around and back to the bus stop, he realized Palo Alto was nothing like Cambridge. For starters it had its own color, its own aura, its own architecture. The towns folk looked different, had their own style of dress and sounded different.

Boarding *"Marguerite"* to take him to campus he couldn't help but notice this very pretty, petite young lady sitting opposite him. She was looking out the window, exuding confidence, and smiling to no one in particular. Looking at her in some way reminded him of himself in some obscure way.

He guessed she was under five feet tall, if that much. Maybe one hundred and five pounds at best… her auburn hair slightly tinted towards favoring the blonde side…

Turning away from the window towards Earl, she asked, "Do I know you? You were looking at me as if you do. I don't think we've ever met, have we?"

"No, I don't think so. I just, just thought you were, I mean you're beautiful."

She smiled…

"Thank you, that is very nice of you to say that. My name is Ellen, Ellen Renee Somers. I'm a student at *Stanford*, well I will be after I register. I'll be pursuing a PhD in Physics… and may I ask who you are?"

In those few seconds a life-long relationship was born.

Ellen Renee Somers was born in a small town just northwest of Encino, California. Though diminutive in size, she had very quickly established herself as the major presence in her family. By he age of five, she was questioning her mother, then her father about the stars at night; how they got to where they were, what they were, why did they shine at night, etc.?

When her parents ran out of answers, it did not dissuade her, she simply asked new questions. "Why did it get dark in evening … where does water come from…where does rain come from?' Questions, questions and more questions. She never tired of asking questions. And though she drove her mother crazy, her father could not get enough of her. An engineer, and amateur astronomer, he relished Ellen's interest, and spent hour after hour with her sharing the magic of mathematics and the configuration of stars.

By the time she was in middle school, her interest in math and science could not be satiated. She declared to her parents that some day she would travel to the moon, and nothing would stop her. Being small in stature only seemed to motivate her to best her peers at everything she undertook. In high school, she excelled in sports, and was especially proficient in track and field. She was so good, that she was named all-state in the marathon, and just missing that recognition in two other events. Once she set her mind on doing something, all those around knew there was no stopping her.

Ellen graduated with high honors from *Rosedale High School*. Received her Bachelor of Science Degree from the *University of California, at Los Angeles*, then went on to achieve a Master's of Science Degree majoring in Physics from the same university.

After teaching two years in the public school system, at the junior high school level, she realized she was put on this earth to do more than try to convince brain-dead teenagers the importance of learning about the world they lived in. She resigned her position, and with her parents financial help, enrolled in *Stanford University* to pursue a doctorate degree in physics, doing most of her research in Astrophysics.

Earl remembered little of the bus ride to campus from the train depot save for the fact that they spoke all the way. Upon arrival they gathered their belongings, wished each other well, and went their separate ways.

But not for long.

A lot of her reminded him of himself. The easy smile; her upright carriage; the sober yet joyous manner in which she spoke about her future; her demeanor… he could not get her out of his thoughts.

Within a week he found out where she lived on campus, and sent a bouquet of flowers to her dorm with a note attached requesting an opportunity to see her again.

❧

Ellen recalled how in that short bus ride, they had spoken of their dreams to carve out a niche for themselves; to make a difference in the world; to travel where few if any had traveled before. Yes he was young, but at the same time he shared her aspirations, seemed extremely bright, and was fun to be with. They were the same height, and she liked not having to look up at someone. Not yet knowing anyone else at the university, she quickly determined that she would start he social life on campus with Earl.

So they met for coffee, and over the next few weeks, coffee became dinner, then dinner became weekends. By the time they were completing their oral exams, and doctoral theses, they were as tight as two peas in a pod.

Here was the missing link in Earl's life. Here was a woman who was an intellectual equal, determined as he was, cute as "all get out," and equal in size and stature. A relationship that could have been made in heaven.

But, after two years, as their student lives were coming to an end, Ellen was ready to move on, though Earl was not. She had no time, nor place in her life for Earl, nor anyone else. Oh, she did care for him, a lot, but nevertheless she had places to see and worlds to conquer. She suggested, if Earl was willing, because she did have feelings for him, she was willing to maintain a close friendship in spirit, and when possible, come together in person. No commitments, just friends with benefits.

Realizing she had her destiny to live, just as he had his, he agreed to her terms, and in he ensuing years, spent one least one weekend a year together.

Yet her ultimatum was hard for Earl to accept. With so little experience in the *World-of-Love* he was devastated. For the first time in his life a woman he loved rejected him…well, didn't quite reject him… but made him feel vulnerable, a new feeling he didn't particularly like. He swore never to allow himself to be put in that position ever again.

And he didn't.

May 20, 2007

8540 Don Quixote Drive

With his glass half empty, Earl's mind returned to his initial decision to study at *Stanford University,* and to contemplate where all the time has gone.

Since achieving the distinction of *Outstanding Scholar at M.I.T.,* and earning a master's degree in both *Engineering and Management Studies,* and in *Brain and Cognitive Science* at the tender age of eighteen, a feat never before accomplished by anyone, *Stanford* had decided that having Earl Starkvisor as a student in one of their doctoral programs was in their best interest, and so they awarded him a full scholarship.

With the knowledge that funding was of no concern, he decided to pursue the degree of *Doctor of Philosophy in Aeronautics and Astronautics* under the auspices of the *Department of Aeronautics and Astronautics,* within the *College of Engineering.*

A game Earl had played with himself on his first trip out west, was to guess the occupation and the number of wealthy people he encountered on the train and in the stations. Since he could never be wrong, it was a wonderful outlet enabling him to use his imagination to the fullest. Because of his analytical mind, and his interest in people, he made the discovery that the prime rationale for coming to his conclusions was the clothing his studies wore. Since he saw most of the same people over the course of a number of days, and kept copious notes as to their attire, he was able with a fair degree of certainty to discern their status in the world. Never having been concerned with his wardrobe, nor what he was or would be wearing, this sudden awareness began to effect the way he would look at the world.

Growing up on hand-me-downs and other clothing his mother somehow acquired for him from second-hand stores, was more than sufficient. At *M.I.T.* he basically wore chino pants, a short or a long sleeve shirt, depending on the season, one of four sweaters his mother had bought for him, and either brown, or white shoes, or high or low back sneakers. He wore this until an item was thread-bare, then it was replaced by a clone.

Suddenly the concept of "you are what your wear" and "dressing for success" took on new meaning for him. He rationalized, that if he judged people by what they wore, then clearly others did the same. The Earl he would become was born at that moment of awareness.

Ultimately, what all this introspection manifested was a melancholy. At times like this he really missed his mom and April...

"Did they think about him as much as he thought of them?

Of course they did, but they had each other, and he was very much alone. He realized he was responsible for their separation, nevertheless he missed them, and right now would have loved to have them with him. He smiled to himself admitting he, the "great" Earl Starkvisor was "a little" homesick, a feeling he didn't know he was capable of, yet was kind of glad he had.

At that moment he knew he was where he was supposed to be.

❧

May 20, 2007

8540 Don Quixote Drive

Starting his second extra, extra dry martini, Earl started to wax poetic…"What fools we mortals be.

Wrong time, wrong place, me thinks it's time to review my notes for this evening's speech. "

"This morning Dr. Bullard, in introducing me mentioned the fact that I am not married, never have been, and probably never will be. He spoke he truth, for I have committed my energies, and my life to the love of teaching. Though I must say I have had many mistresses and liaisons along the way, namely: Biology, Chemistry, Astro-Physics, and Nuclear Biology. I have no regrets, well…maybe one…or maybe two."

That should get a laugh, it always has.

"Honored guests, the opportunity to stand before you, and recite a few words of gratitude for being awarded the mantle of one of the 2009 Outstanding Teachers at Brookside University is as rewarding to me as it is humbling. To have been so fortunate to be able to do what I love, and to love what I do, is rare in our society, and sad to say becoming more and more difficult to achieve.

The first lecture I give to new students at the beginning of each new semester, has been given the endearing title, Dr. Starkvisor's 3C'sT&D, the five dreaded letters. On some occasions, and only behind my back, Dr. Starkvisor becomes Dr. Strangevisor; student sense of humor… not funny, but to be expected.

After many years of practice I have gotten quite good at lifting my left arm which had been resting on the podium, and shooting it up to my shoulder, like this. Then 'poker-faced.' I slowly and meticulously use my right hand to lower my left arm back to the podium, and stare ahead. This is usually followed by a few seconds of silence until the class realizes I am spoofing Peter Sellers memorable portrayal of Dr. Strangelove, and at the same time joking with them. Thus the realization that I can laugh at myself puts the entire class at ease.

Ladies and gentlemen, if I have to say it myself, and I have to say it to myself, I… am truly a sweet, kind lovable person in spite of what has, and is, being said about me. I am not a tyrant! I believe my reputation emanates from my bald head, precise manner and the fact that on one occasion or two, I can be dictator-like.

Alas and alack, those are the reasons I believe these accusations have been fostered. It is a charge I categorically deny. But will readily admit… quite possibly on rare occasions, I can be willful… maybe once or twice, directive… but authoritarian, **never!**"

Allowing the audience a moment to realize they are being spoofed, he then continues.

"I would like to get serious for a moment. The teaching/learning process is serious business, but should not preclude being enjoyable. Making learning exciting, profound and meaningful is my responsibility, and I believe it should be the responsibility of every teacher worth his or her weight in salt. At the same time, it is the students' responsibility to attend to learning the content of my classes. This is called the participatory process.

To that end, I have developed the 3C'sT&D.

They are introduced in my first lecture to my students on the first day of class. 3C'sT&D represent the five elements I believe are necessary to become a successful scientist, and a successful citizen.

They are:

1. **C**reativity: the need to be able to combine ideas from a multitude of sources. To filter them through one's ability to perceive and ideate, and bring them into the cold, harsh light of reality. To encounter virgin territory without fear, to create pathways never before seen, to utilize the opportunity to do something as it has never been thought of doing before.

2. **C**ommitment: the willingness to surrender some of your freedom to pursue a long-term goal. The determination to succeed regardless of the obstacles thrown in your path. The ability to dive into strange waters, with the full confidence that you will surface with more knowledge then before.

3. **C**ompassion: one cannot achieve greatness without compassion. It is the need to share a deep sensitivity to the sufferings, and aspirations of others. Be it Martin Luther King, Buddha or Jesus, they all are revered today because they shared a common thread. They had compassion.

4. **T**eamwork: the knowledge that you need the talents and the cooperation of others to bring to fruition a major project. It doesn't matter how brilliant you are, you can't do it alone. Think of the game of football. The greatest quarterback alive cannot catch his own passes, and without blockers a running back can't gain yards. It is also the realization that when the team wins, everyone wins.

5. **D**rive: the ability to self-propel an engine that never quits. Everything you start, you finish, then start all over again. Visualize your goals and establish a plan to succeed; if plan A doesn't work, go immediately to plan B. If plan B doesn't work, go to plan C. The word failure is not part of your vocabulary.

I have never accused myself of being a poet. Nevertheless, I do believe these words cut the chaff off the grain, and are the essence of success.

The global economy is a difficult age to be entering the workforce. More importantly, to be embarking upon a world in need of citizenship is equally as difficult, and could be extremely fearful. You, tomorrow's graduates must correct the mistakes and abuses of my generation to enable your children to reap the benefits of our great planet.

I beg you to step forward, to slay the evils of bigotry and greed, and allow me and your loved ones, to sit back with pride, smile and say, that was my student! That's my son! That's my daughter!

Thank you again honored guests for your patience in allowing this semi-old bachelor to ramble, and for your graciousness in listening."

Book Three
Nan Alderage-Gates

May 20, 2007

110 Atridge Place (a moderate 1,800 sq. ft. town house in the suburb of Wentwood, twenty miles south of Brookside University)

"Mom, Rose, I'm going to take a shower. I'm exhausted. Mom, I will really miss you and Rose not being at the dinner tonight. I know you will be there with me in spirit, but nevertheless, I'll miss your physical presence. It will sadden me, looking out at the audience, and not seeing your faces. I owe you both so much."

From the other room Nan heard her mother, "Nan honey, you will be fine. This is your day. You have been fighting for this recognition all your life, and today you received it. This is your day. You don't need us there. It is *you* they want to see. Enjoy the recognition. Revel in the fact, that in a man's world, you made it to the top. I, we could not be more proud of you. Now go out there this evening, and 'knock em dead'

Tomorrow you can tell Rose and I all about it."

Nan smiled, and once in the shower, with the hot water pouring down on her body, she began to think about her mom, her dad, and the journey she had been on for so many years.

Nan Alderage-Gates, the oldest of five children born to Naomi Alderage and Paul Gates, was a disappointment her father never got over. He had wanted a son. Yet she knew he loved her, or at least thought he loved her, after all, fathers were supposed to love all their children even if they were daughters. She could swear he said he loved her at least once or twice a year, although she had trouble recalling the exact times she thought he had said it. Well she gave him credit for trying. Nan knew that no matter how hard he pretended it didn't matter, he could not hide his disappointment that his first born was a girl. If that was not punishment enough, as it turned out, Nan was the oldest of five girls.

Paul Gates, the oldest of three sons of a Baptist preacher was initially being groomed by his father to follow in his footsteps. After discovering his son had no interest in books, wasn't comfortable being around more than two people at a time, and only exhibited joy being outdoors and inter-acting with the earth, he decided he would teach the boy farming skills. At least this way the boy could keep himself alive. His father's decision made Paul happy, for he didn't have many friends, didn't want many friends, hated the thought of having to work for someone, and had no interest in being social.

At church on Sunday, Paul would sneak out when people were shouting out their hymns, saying their amen's, and walk down to the creek which abutted the church's property. Careful not to get himself dirty, he would find himself a remnant of a tree to sit on, and a branch to carve with his trusty little pen knife.

It was on a warm Sunday in July when he met Naomi.

Naomi was the only daughter of her doting parents Jasmine, and John Alderage. She did have eight brothers which was a good thing, for as the brothers got older they all worked with their Dad on the family farm.

Naomi, became Mom II and spent most of her time helping in the kitchen, and doing the family laundry. Nine working males made for hard labor for the only two females in the family.

Life was not easy for the Alderage clan, each member of the family labored long and hard to fulfill their obligations. At the same time, Jasmine and John's attitude and outlook on life made every day a special day. From early morn, until she retired for the evening, Jasmine wore a warm smile while humming a variety of tunes. Regardless of any misfortune that occurred, she never let it dampen her spirit.

As much as John Alderage adored his wife, his only daughter brought a sparkle to his eyes.

Growing up with two such wonderful parents instilled within Naomi a deep love for them, and a calmness that would transcend the madness of the world, and serve her well as she aged.

"Hi there, what ya doin?"

Paul looked up and saw what he thought was the prettiest gal he had ever seen.

"My name is Naomi Alderage. I live up the road apiece on Barrington Road. Aren't you Reverend Gates' son?

"Yup."

"What are you doing there?"

"Carving."

"Can I see?"

"Yup."

"Not bad. What is it?"

"A walking stick."

"Shouldn't it be longer?"

"Maybe, but that's the size of the stick I found."

"Okay, then I guess it's fine."

Within six months of that auspicious beginning, Paul and Naomi, meeting almost every Sunday were quite sure they were meant for each other. Being of marrying age, with no other prospects in the vicinity, both sets of parents reluctantly agreed. Paul's father gave his son five acres of his homestead on which Paul would set up his farm. Naomi's father and her eight brothers volunteered to build them a house and a barn on the newly acquired land. Naomi was always fascinated by how things went together, an interest which eventually manifested itself into a career for her oldest daughter, watched and carefully supervised the construction.

Naomi Alderage was born seven miles down the road from the Gates family home. Grateful for her family upbringing, and proud to be an "Alderage" she swore never to give up the Alderage name. A vow which almost ended her marriage to Paul before it had a chance to begin. In that day and time, a woman not only gave up her name when she got married, but swore obedience to her husband. Nevertheless Naomi would not budge. She was willing to take Paul to her bed, and share his name, but not give up her own. Tiring of these minor spats about a name, Naomi gave her future husband an ultimatum; "take me and my middle name, or call it quits right now!" Paul Gates finally realizing the inanity of his position, assessed the situation. No where else was he going to find a woman as pretty in face and form as Naomi; no where else was he going to find a woman as strong and as gentle as Naomi, so his decision to take her as his wife, along with her name was a no-brainer. "If she wants to keep her damn last name, let her." In actuality, it didn't really matter a hoot to him, because all he ever called her was "Ma" anyway, just like his father called his mother, and his grandfather called his grandmother.

Though not as effusive as his father, nor overt in showing his emotions, Paul had his own ways of showing love. Some days Naomi would go into the kitchen to prepare breakfast, she would find on the kitchen table a gift of a small carving, other days she would find one of her chores completed, and most days Paul would ask her if she needed him to do anything for her.

Eleven months later Nan Alderage Gates was born, and for the first time since they were married, Paul Gates was dismayed. He had wanted a son, especially to be his eldest. Why he felt this way could not be answered. As his father's oldest son, it was true he carried his father's name; but as a son to work along side his father, he was a failure. And if a son was to be considered a resource, once again, a failure. No his father got no pleasure, nor benefits from his oldest son.

But a girl? Paul Gates could not fathom what he would do with a girl child. It was a clear as day he was not comfortable with women, no less little girls. He tried to keep his disappointment to himself, but was not successful. He spent more time in the field, leaving a little earlier and returning a little later. Most evenings he spent idly carving away on the porch, nothing specific, simply carving. Naomi, thrilled to have a child, especially to have one as beautiful as her daughter, not used to much attention, was too busy mothering her child to notice any change in her husband.

With the ensuing birth of four more daughters, Paul found more and more reasons to stay out in the fields longer, and longer. And when at home, he was almost a total stranger to his children.

Naomi, this wonderful, gentle, loving woman never took notice of her husband's behavior. Life in the Alderage Gates home was, "doing business as usual."

Growing up Nan adored her father. This gentle, quiet giant who slaved away in the fields every day. As she got older, and more responsible, she would try to help him, but was rejected continuously. Wanting his love so desperately, she emulated everything he did. She tried to walk like him, and speak like him. She told her mother she hated doing household chores, she would prefer to help her father in the fields. Regardless of her efforts, nothing seemed to change or move him. Without ever understanding why, she tried the very hard to become the son her father never had.

The results of her efforts were that she could do the manual labor required of any farm hand, fix any tractor around the farm, and handle herself in any kind of argument. What she didn't succeed in doing was getting her father's approval. In a tribute to her tenacity, she never stopped trying.

All through her junior and senior year of high school her math and science teacher, Mrs. Greene had encouraged her to make plans to continue her education, telling her she was gifted in both areas. Other than thanking her for her kind words, and sharing with her teacher that she probably inherited her interest from her mom, Nan thought little of the advice. She joked about the fact that she didn't get her mother's good looks, so an interest in science and math was better than nothing. Always adding in a prideful manner that she did get her height and muscularity from her father.

It was in the Spring, right before planting season, when she got into a shouting match with her father at the dinner table. It seemed she couldn't wait to share the fact that she had to re-repair the seeder, after her father had used the wrong bolt, a bolt which sheared the minute the engine was started, and if it wasn't for her, that valuable piece of equipment would have been rendered unusable.

When her remarks elicited no response from her father, she arose from her seat, pointed at her father and accused him of screwing up more than this one time. Then she rubbed salt into the open wound bragging that if it wasn't for her, the entire farm would be in trouble.

Her father's face turned beet red. He put his spoon down on the table, looked Nan straight in her eyes, and said, "Mind your mouth girl, this is a dinner table. Now sit down and eat your food."

But Nan was on a roll now.

"No dad, I won't sit down! Why, after all these years, why can't you say something nice about me. Why can't you admit you need me, if not need me, then at least say to me that I am a big help to you? Why can't you ever just say "thank you? Why is it everything I do, you trivialize with a scornful look, and a few shakes of the head?" Why is it you've never hugged me? Am I that ugly? Why is it you've never said, "hey, hey big daughter, I love you! Do you realize you have never ever, touched me, or kissed me? You can't even shake my hand. Could it be that you are simply incapable of showing any human emotion?"

When Nan completed her tirade, the room was absolutely still. With all eyes staring at Nan's father, he slowly arose from his seat, turned to Nan, and said, "I'll do better than shake your hand young lady."

With those words he swatted Nan across her mouth with a mighty backhanded slap. The noise sounded as if a bomb exploded in the room. As she tumbled to the floor, she began crying, not tears of physical pain, but tears of embarrassment and shame. As her mother and sisters knelt to help her, the one person she wanted love and respect from, more than anyone else in the world, her father, looked away from her, and stomped out of the house, slamming the front door shut as he went.

At that moment she decided she would leave this household as soon as she could.

It was an epiphany.

Arriving early at school on Monday, almost an hour before classes began, she waited in front of Mrs. Greene's office, her science teacher. She was the only person in the world who on a consistent basis, had praised her and befriended her. One look at Nan and she quickly ushered her into her office knowing intuitively that something was very wrong.

Thinking herself as able to handle any situation, Nan surprised herself when she broke down in front of Mrs. Greene. It surprised her even more that she continued crying the entire time she was explaining her reasons for being there. Nan always thought of herself as tough. How tough could she really be if she cried like a silly girl? As the tears continued to flow Mrs. Greene got up from her chair, went over to Nan, hugged her, and comforted her. The physical contact from another human being was like food to someone who is starving. For the first time in Nan's life, she felt loved, and safe.

After explaining what had occurred, Nan asked, no begged, Mrs. Greene for help in applying to college, for it was, in her mind, the only passage out of the misery of her home. Since she didn't have any money, and could not depend on support from her parents, she wondered if it would be possible for her to help Nan arrange for a loan, find a part time job, and/or possibly guide her in applying for a scholarship.

With Mrs. Greene's guidance and counseling, she was soon accepted to State's Teacher's College, less than a hundred miles from her home, and awarded a scholarship. Prior to Nan's high school graduation, Mrs. Greene hired her to do yard work, and home maintenance three hours a day after school and for six hours on Saturday. With this money earned and under Mrs. Greene's guidance, Nan opened a bank account and learned how to be frugal.

Only after she received the official letter of acceptance into the state college, and armed with her bank book, did she inform her mother of her plans. Not knowing what to expect, Nan was surprised at her mother's reaction. She hugged her, really hugged her, and told her how proud she was of her achievements. Asked if she informed her father, Nan replied, "no!"

"I have not spoken one word to him since he hit me. I hate him. I really don't care if he lives or dies! And I would greatly appreciate it if you didn't tell him a word about this. He doesn't give a damn about me, and I don't give a damn about him."

"That's not right Nan. He is your father and deserves your respect. He loves you, he really does, only he doesn't know how to show it. He has told me how sorry he was about slapping you. It was the first time in his life he ever hit anyone. He is a good man, a good provider, he just doesn't know how to be affectionate, or share his emotions."

"Mom, nothing you say will change the way I feel. I hate him, and can't wait to be out of this house. I love you and my sisters, and I will miss you all, but him, no. I will not ask him for anything, nor will I have anything to do with him."

As summer came to a close, and the leaves began to change color, Nan packed all her belongings into the two suitcases she had purchased at the second-hand store in town, and said her good-byes to her mother and sisters. As she left her house and walked to the gate that defined the farm's front boundary, she noticed in the distance her father watching her, sitting upon his tractor. As she turned towards him, he looked away.

On her way to the bus station she stopped at Mrs. Greene's house to say good-bye. Mrs. Greene seemed to be waiting for her on her front porch. How she has sensed she was coming, Nan didn't know, but it was clear she had expected her, for she had a lunch bag filled with two tuna salad sandwiches, a small container of milk, and a chocolate cup cake. In Mrs. Greene's other hand was a beautifully wrapped gift box.

"Honey, this is for you. It's personal, so don't open it until you are alone, and when you do, think of me." With that Mrs. Greene gave her an extended hug, holding her very tight. Nan stood there flabbergasted, not knowing what to do, so she did nothing, but thought to herself… that was nice.

Nan did very well at "State". She majored in Science, with a minor in Math. Her cumulative grade point average over the four years in school was a 3.8; she was named the school's outstanding scholar, and was asked to deliver the valedictory speech at graduation. She had proven herself more than competent in the academic arena, and had developed the confidence that she would become successful in any competitive environment she decided upon. Yes, she would and could excel. She would show her father that she was not only as good as any man, but better!

As her career choices were narrowing down it became much easier to choose her next academic environment. To that end had applied and been accepted into the *Rensselaer Polytechnic Institute's (R.P.I.)* master's program, for she had finally decided engineering would be her life's work, and *R.P.I.* was one of the best programs in the country.

She hadn't been home in four years, although her mother had visited her on two occasions, and promised she would be there for graduation. Her sisters came to visit her three to four times a year. Those visits were always fun, and she was amazed at how fast they had grown, and what beautiful young women they had become. She was content except for one nagging issue… her father. She knew that she didn't hate him. She had said that in anger and frustration. It was her stubbornness that impelled her to continue saying it. But deep in her heart she really loved him, and for some reason, she missed him. With distance, she had soon realized, that in many ways they were more similar than different. These four years, living on her own, had shown her to be a loner. She was very comfortable being with herself, and learned that the less you depended on people, the more in control you were.

Graduation was a benchmark. Like all benchmarks in a life-time, it was an opportunity to re-visit the past. To evaluate the why and the why-not's of the past. To feel good about one's achievements, analyze the mistakes and plan not to make similar ones in the future.

An outcome of all this introspection was her decision to go home that summer, practice forgiveness, and re-activate her relationship with her father.

Yes, life was good. She was closer towards becoming the person she wanted to be. She had discovered it wasn't her lack of physical endowments that turned men away, it was her attitude. She just was not interested in having a relationship with a man. The few times she had dated, necked and even petted, didn't do anything for her. She would return to her room, and begin to recall Mrs. Greene's passionate hug. Soon the awkwardness of the evening's date would disappear, and was replaced with a smile. Then she was able to fall asleep.

It was in her junior year when she allowed her consciousness to verbalize that she liked the company of women more then men. She was comfortable with women, and she discovered that she liked touching and being touched by women. This awareness was a result of her taking an art history class in Fall semester.

Lauren Volmer was the professor teaching *French Painting in the Nineteenth Century*. Mrs. Greene, Nan's high school teacher had introduced her to the world of Art through the numerous reproductions of paintings hung all over her home; paintings by Monet (the hay stack series), Manet's *Sejuener sur l'herbe*, Degas' *A Ballet seen from an Opera Box, and* Renior's *Moulin de la Galette*. When Mrs. Greene wasn't talking about science or math, she was sure to talk about her love of 19th Century French painting. Nan thought this would be an opportunity to gain some insight into her mentor's love.

Seated, chatting with some other students about registering for the class, the bell rang, and a tall, slender, woman entered the room and walked up to the podium. Though interested in learning about the History of Art, that day all she could do was stare at the professor. The woman was dazzling. Her figure beautiful, slim, but in her mind perfectly proportioned. She had long, copper-toned hair, radiating out like the rays of the sun. If asked what she learned that day, all she would be able to say was that Professor Volmer had this habit of pushing a few strands of hair that continually fell on her forehead towards the back of her ears, and doing it with a beautiful elegant hand. Her professor also had exquisite blue-green eyes, long slender fingers with perfectly shaped ruby red nails. She had style!

After class Nan shyly approached Professor Volmer and asked her if she would mind if she taped her lecture, for her note taking ability was not as well developed as she would have liked. To Nan's surprise, Professor Volmer said she *did* mind, and went on to say she believed her lectures were her professional property, and some day she was planning to use them and write a book. She suggested if Nan had trouble taking notes, she would speak to a student in class who she knew was an excellent note-taker, and ask if she would share them. Nan thanked her and walked out of class thinking Professor Lauren Volmer was the most beautiful woman she had ever seen.

The first exam of her Art class came in the fourth week. The material it covered dealt with the invention of photography and how it effected painting; a review of Neoclassicism, Romanticism and Realism, and the lives and the work of Honore Daumier, and Gustave Courbet. All of which was covered in depth in the classroom.

The following Monday Professor Volmer handed back the graded tests in class. Nan was pleased to see a 98 written on the top of the first page. Written below the 98 was, "You did extremely well. Please see me after class."

Not expecting anything but a grade, Nan became a little nervous about the meaning of the attached note. Waiting patiently until all the other students left the room she approached the teacher's desk. "Excuse me Professor Volmer, did I do something wrong? I thought I did pretty good." Looking up from a memo she was writing, Professor Volmer smiled and assured Nan she was doing fine and, in fact, had received the highest grade in the class.

"No no, it has nothing to do with class." Professor Volmer explained she was having a dinner party that Friday, and wondered if Nan would like to come. She said there would be six or seven other students, and some other faculty. Stunned at the invitation, all she could do was stand there and shake her head yes.

As Nan discovered later, all the guests were women.

Professor Volmer's home was nothing like Nan had ever seen before. Set back about one hundred feet from the road, in a rural area, not far from school. Nan encountered a home which seemed to be composed of a series of long and narrow vertical boxes which. working together, created a much larger shape, a shape which epitomized elegance and solidarity.

The most striking feature of the house Nan thought, was the pattern of shadows which gave the overall feeling that the building was even longer than it was. Low, long and dramatic but welcoming, was the way Nan described it in a letter to Mrs. Greene. Never having seen a cantilevered roof before, not thinking about the use of steel beams in construction, Nan felt a little leery about entering the home thinking the roof could collapse any moment. Nevertheless, her excitement quickly overcame her naïve apprehensions.

The interior of the home was as spectacular as the exterior. The entrance foyer leading to the living room was marked by a massive chimney/fireplace which occupied and entire wall. To the left of the foyer was the library which led out to the cantilevered-roofed terrace. To the right, an enormous dining room. In the center of which was a built-in table surrounded by chairs. She later discovered the table could accommodate eighteen people.

To the left of the dining room was a huge working kitchen, which, at the time Nan saw it, was housed by three busy working women in white wearing elaborate, tall white hats. French doors led out to the courtyard, which was rich with color and texture. She was later informed, that to maintain the gardens a full-time gardener was employed.

The scientist/mathematician in Nan was intrigued by how the design of the house merged simplicity with complexity; strong with soft, and formal with informal.

The dinner was fantastic. It began with a lobster cocktail served in ice-filled crystal bowls. The main-course, *Beef Wellington,* was served with sweet and sour baby onions, zesty baby carrots and baby corn. Each plate was individually prepared and looked beautiful enough to be a still-life painting, Nan was hesitant to dig in, fearing she would ruin the image.

The *Caesar salad,* was prepared at the table-side by a server whose hands moved as if she were conducting a symphony. All in attendance later commented not only on the lady's deftness, but the savory flavor the salad imbued.

The wine served, was a chilled *Chardonnay*. Not only was this the most elegant meal Nan had ever participated in, but it was the first time she had tasted wine. She loved the taste, so much, she asked for her glass to be refilled often. Feeling a little light-headed, but wonderful, she just sat back and enjoyed.

Dessert consisted of the most delicious carrot cake Nan had tasted in her life! It was served with demitasse, a strong coffee the likes Nan had never before experienced.

About 10:30 p.m. as conversation began to wind down, and the students began to go, Nan suddenly realized she would be the last student there. Embarrassed at what she thought was a social gaffe, she quickly retrieved her coat from a small coat room, and went to say thank you, and good-by to the host.

"Nan, please don't go, I really haven't had a chance to talk with you." She put her arm over Nan's shoulder and led her back into the living room.

"Please be patient with me just a few moments longer, my other guests are leaving, and I would like to bid them good night." Before leaving the room, this elegant tall woman whose hair looked redder than before probably because it was contrasted by a stunning, sleeveless, v-necked white silk dress that looked like she was poured into it, gave Nan another glass of wine, smiled at her and left the room.

It took about ten minutes for her last guest to leave. At first Nan just sat back in the easy chair, slowly sipping her wine, enjoying her first "buzz," and admiring the precision and beauty of her surroundings. After a few minutes she began to feel uneasy, and began to perspire.

When Nan's host re-entered the room, Nan jumped to her feet almost spilling her wine. "Professor Volmer, I'm so sorry, I, I, I,..."

"Please relax, relax, in fact I instructed told you to do so, didn't I? And since we are not at school, I would prefer you call me Lauren."

Looking right into Nan's eyes, and smiling the warmest, most welcoming smile, she took Nan's hand and guided her to the couch. Nan noticed for the first time that her host was not wearing a bra, and her nipples were outlined by the softness of the dress material. Realizing she was starring at her host's breasts, she became flushed and began to stammer which was interrupted by her host asking her what she thought of the people gathered there this evening?

"Well, I, I, I noticed everyone here was female. I've seen two of the girls in classes, and I've seen two of the teachers in the halls. Everyone seemed to be very nice, good conversationalists, and very friendly. I think that's about it."

"What would you say, if I told you all of my guests were gay?" Nan's body became rigid, her mouth opened a bit even though no words came out of it, and her eyes widened.

Lauren's smile changed slightly noticing how uncomfortable Nan was becoming. "Well Nan I asked you a simple question. I know you are a very bright young lady, in fact, I think you are the brightest student in my class. So I'll ask you again what if I told you they are all lesbians?"

"I guess it is okay for people to be gay. I mean…, I mean… I can only guess, because I don't have a lot of experience. I don't date much, I know I dislike being pawed at, and gawked at. And boys can be such jerks at times. The truth is that I've always been more comfortable with girls. I have four younger sisters, and being the oldest I always looked out for them. If anyone gave them a hard time, especially the boys, I took care of it. I can handle myself well; even here at school boys don't try to hit on me. In my freshman year some fraternity jerk tried to get a little too personal with me, so I decked him. Since then, I'm pretty much left to myself."

As Nan was now talking non-stop, Lauren was again refilling Nan's glass, then interrupted her. "I've noticed you are very comfortable with yourself. You walk tall, are poised, and as I mentioned bright. From where I stand it looks like people respect you."

Lauren noticed the wine bottle was empty. With a warm engaging smile, she said, "Well, no problem, I have others chilling in the refrigerator. Excuse me for one moment, I'll be right back." Arising effortlessly from the couch, Lauren walked into the kitchen. As she did, Nan noticed the elegance of her host's gait, the subtle movement of fabric against her hips, and the habitual way she kept tossing her head to rearrange her hair.

The words she heard her teacher say comforted Nan and made her feel good. No one had ever said those kind words to her before. Except for Mrs. Greene, of course, who had complimented her lots of times. Thinking of Mrs. Greene brought about a soft smile, especially remembering her good-bye hug. With those thoughts in her head she began to relax a little.

Exiting from the kitchen with a newly opened bottle of champagne in an ice bucket, Nan noticed how the material of her host's dress outlined her legs, literally clinging to her body.

Suddenly Nan became conscious of the direction of her thoughts. "Oh my God, what am I thinking. I like boys. Of course I like boys, at least I think I like boys. But Mrs. Greene…, all the guests here tonight are gay…" A thousand thoughts and questions raced through Nan's troubled mind. "Could Lauren

Volmer be gay? Does she think I am gay? Could I be, and not know it?"

Her host placed the ice bucket on the coffee table in front of the couch and sat down next to Nan. Her knees barely touching Nan's thigh. Shifting in place, perhaps to get a little more comfortable, she unpinned her hair, tossed her head back, and with a sigh, ran her fingers through it. Nan could not take her eyes off of her. She noticed her cleavage, and could discern the lines of her breasts. Nan could feel her own breasts begin to tingle and her nipples harden. With a start she realized that what she really wanted to do was to caress her teacher's hair and kiss her lips.

Then Nan became aware that her host looking at her. "I'm, I, I'm sorry, I, I don't know what to say. I've never felt this way before. I, I think I may be a little drunk, but I just think you are beautiful, and the most sexy person I have ever met."

All her host did was to patiently allow for her to continue talking while she continued to smile. It was if Lauren Volmer, by letting her hair fall free, became softer and more intimate. After saying what she did, baring her soul, a great weight was removed from her, and Nan sat back, leaned her head against the back of the sofa and closed her eyes. She did not know what was going to happen next, but at this point she didn't care. She felt relieved and in inexplicable way excited. Knowing her timing was impeccable, Lauren Volmer gently placed one arm around Nan's shoulder, reached into her blouse and caressed her breast, at the same time gently kissing Nan's lips.

"Nan, let's go upstairs to my bedroom. I give you my word, I will not do anything to you that you don't want. I just want to hold you, and touch you."

Nan's could feel her body radiating heat, as her breath quickened. The wine she'd consumed eroded any hesitancy she may have had. Unable to think of anything other than Lauren's beauty and her desirable body, nodded, and hand in hand they went up the stairs and into Lauren's bedroom.

Walking into that space was like entering a Hollywood set. The room itself had to be 25' by 35' with plush white wall-to-wall carpeting. The white walls displayed large (30"x40") Abstract Expressionistic prints. On the wall to her right hung Hans Hofmann's *The Gate,* with its stark red and yellow rectangles popping off the surface. On the same wall separated by a door that led into a walk-in closet was Robert Motherwell's *Elegy to the Spanish Republic No.34..* Though totally different, the prints were equally powerful. On the wall to Nan's left hung Barnett Newman's Color Field paintings, *Vir Heroicus Sublimis.* Near it hung Ad Reinhardt's *Abstract Painting Blue;* an absolute perfect choice to share a space with Newman's work.

The wall opposite the entry door was designed with clearstory windows from one side of the room to the other. At that very moment, the moonlight entering the room through the clearstory windows was magical, not only creating an aura-like effect, but illuminating a copy of Picasso's *La Joie de vivre,* in all its 47 ¼ by 98 ½" size. The painting with its flat-color planes, depict centaurs piping music with playful goats skipping playfully around a beautiful nymph whose sensuous black hair floats in the air framing her head, while she dances in the breeze. The painting, copied by a former art student, was positioned to simulate a headboard for the king sized bed, which was covered in pink satin sheets and a variety of pillows.

Nan was awestruck! A dream, she knew she had to be in a dream. The entire evening, the emotions and sensations speeding through her body, all of it a wonderful dream.

With great patience, Lauren did not want to rush things. Lauren allowed Nan all the time she needed to look around, relax and feel comfortable then gently guided Nan to her bed, and slowly undressed her, and then herself. She next began to slowly caress Nan's body. First she kissed her neck, then moved her lips to Nan's breasts as her hands gently stroked her abdomen. Adding just a slight amount of pressure, she parted Nan's legs, and stroked her thighs. Nan felt she was floating above the bed, a voyeur of her own new journey."

Lauren was now licking and kissing Nan's thighs then moved higher and higher. The feelings she was experiencing made her involuntarily cry out, "Oh God!" This gave the word "erotic" a new meaning. Nan could only cry out in ecstasy. Urged on by Lauren's soft murmuring, Nan began to touch in return, the soft, silky skin of her lover, until both began to experience a series of spasms, shuddered, and with soft moans climaxed.

Covering Nan's body and hers with a sheet, Lauren laid Nan's head upon her arm, and with her right hand began to caress her hair. They stayed in that warm embrace and drifted off to sleep.

Nan woke up during the night and, for a moment, wondered where she was. Slowly she lifted the sheet and in the moonlight stared at Lauren's naked body. It was ravishing. Snuggling close to her, with tentative, gentle strokes Nan began to caress Lauren's body. Suddenly, as if awakened from a dream, Nan sat up. She felt extremely awkward at her forwardness in touching her teacher's body, and did not know what to do next. Not wanting to make a fool of herself and at the same time not wanting this time to end. Lauren, in a soft, gentle voice whispered, "it's okay, it's okay, it's okay." Encouraged by words, Nan once again began caressing and kissing Lauren's body. She placed soft, lingering kisses on her mouth, on the tip of her chin, the corners of her eyes. Nan's entire body coursed with a delicious waves of pleasure. She was floating with it, burning with her desire, and she heard herself begin to moan.

Aroused, Lauren arose, pressed her lips against Nan's, and stroked her breast. Bodies rubbing, hips pressing, hands touching, searching, stroking, caressing. Nan then became the aggressor. Being alive at this moment, her senses rampant, and being in control engendered an energy Nan did not know existed. She gently pressed her teacher down on her back, and found her breasts. Her mouth began to explore Lauren's body with her tongue. Within moments after spreading her teacher's legs and penetrating her body, Lauren had an orgasm so powerful it shook the bed. The rest of the night, and early into the next morning they took turns pleasing each other.

Until she graduated, Nan visited Lauren's home on an average of once a month, usually on a Friday returning to her dorm on Saturday. Both teacher and student were totally satisfied with the relationship. Lauren had found a partner and willing student, and Nan had found great pleasure and relief in discovering that her sexuality was another part of her, of who she was and she felt no shame.

May 20, 2007

110 Atridge Place

Relaxed and refreshed after her shower, Nan returned to the living room. Rose Anne not wanting to disturb Nan had left her a note informing her that she was helping Nan's mom change and get ready for her evening activities which included first, a cup of hot tea, and then a front row seat in front of the television set. A routine her mother had become quite comfortable with.

"Rose Anne, Rose Anne, I do love you. Where would I be without you? But I think before dwelling on you, me, us… I'd best review what I will say this evening."

Retrieving her briefcase from the entrance foyer table, she removed her notes for this evenings speech, poured herself a glass of Chardonnay (the flavor of the wine brought back fond memories), got comfortable on the living room sofa, and started reading.

"Ladies and gentlemen, working with and admiring Professor MacKeon, I knew he would be sharing with you profound thoughts written by one or more of the great writers of the past. Also having the same regards for Professor Starkvisor I knew he would be speaking of profundity and pragmatism. Professor Gill, well… no one including Professor Gill knows in advance what he is going to say.

Pause, smile

The amazing thing about him is when, and after he says something it usually makes a lot of sense and is quite profound. Being simply a not-so-little country girl, I'd just like to say hi, and it feels really good being here.

(pause a second time, give them time to smile and sit back in their chairs, hopefully.)

Albert Einstein has said, "the gift of fantasy has meant more to me than my talent for absorbing knowledge." He has also said that "imagination is more important than knowledge." And lastly, as my hero advised, "you can not solve a problem with the same kind of thinking that created it."

His words have been the guiding principles captaining our college's development into the forefront of today's technology.

Some of my proudest moments here at the university have been the development and recognition of Nanolithography, first as a science and now into a full-fledged major. From its birth, which can be traced back to 1958, when the first primitive integrated circuit was created, to now where the limitless boundaries of Nanolithography are fully recognized.

The future is now and here at *Brookside University*, and Nanolithography is leading the way. In just a few years we have assumed a leadership role in scientific expertise, and the center of development for/of qualified professionals. We continue to work hard to re-establish up-state New York as the center for technological development and career training.

There is a story I tell my students about Itzhak Perlman, the great violinist. I'd like to share it with you today.

On November 18, 1995, he came on stage at the *Avery Fisher Hall* at *Lincoln Center* in New York City. The audience was hushed as they watched him walk out on stage and towards his seat. Having been struck with polio as a child, he was wearing braces on both legs, and walked using the assistance of two crutches. Majestically he seated himself, put the crutches on the floor, arranged his feet, locked the braces in place, picked up his violin, adjusted it under his chin and nodded at the conductor to proceed.

As he began playing, no more than a few bars into the symphony, one of the strings on his violin broke. It sounded like gunfire to the hushed crowd, and endlessly reverberated around the auditorium. The deafening silence that ensued could be heard and felt by all in attendance. The master simply sat there, not moving a muscle.

What Perlman did next was nothing less than a miracle. He paused, looked up, closed his eyes, then signaled the conductor to begin again. The orchestra began and Perlman played his music with such passion, such power and with such purity, it was unheard of. Now everyone knows a person cannot play a symphonic work with just three strings, but that night Perlman refused to know that.

The audience in awe and wonder watched him modulate, change, and recompose the piece in his head. To some it sounded as if he was de-tuning the strings to get new sounds from them, tones they had never made before. At the conclusion of the piece, there was an absolute silence. Slowly from every corner of the auditorium there arose the sound, the uproar of people cheering and applauding.

Itzhak Perlman simply smiled, wiped the sweat from his brow, raised his bow to quiet the audience, then in a non-boastful, quiet, reverent tone said, "you know, sometimes it is the artist's task to find out how much music he can make when things are not the way he would want them to be. To make do with what you have, and not worry about what you don't have."

And so I tell my students, in the fast-paced, often bewildering world of the 21ˢᵗ Century, we must challenge ourselves to utilize all of what we have, and all of what we didn't remember we had.

I am grateful to the faculty and administration for giving me the opportunity to head the development team in leading the way for Nano-breakthroughs in the future. Being both a scientist and an engineer, having experience in government, private industry and public research facilities, I have been able, with the help of my colleagues to help make a great university into an even greater one, and one that will continue to grow for many decades to come.

And so I gratefully accept this award on behalf of the faculty and students of the College of Nano-technology, Robotics and Computer Based Technologies.

Thank you."

Looking up from her notes, she saw Rose Ann watching her.

"What do you think Rose Ann? Do you think they will like it?

I wonder what my father would think seeing me up there before thousands of people on the same stage as the Vice President of the United States? Do you think he would be proud of me, even deign to shake my hand?

Well, no matter, he is gone, but we are still very much alive."

Arising from the sofa, she went to the kitchen, poured Rose Ann a glass of wine, handed it to her and said, "To you Rose Ann Tedico, my loving partner for the last twenty-five years. You are my rock, my soul mate and my best friend.

I love you."

❧

Literally, and figuratively Nan bumped into Rose Anne Tedico the first day of classes at *Purdue University*. Both had been advised that *Purdue* was one of the best places in the country for them to study, for it would allow them to achieve their desired career goals at a highly respected university. An environment that fostered intellectually and demographically diverse programs, while encouraging the feeling of a small, but special community of scholars.

And so both weaved their way to the mid-west.

Having arrived on campus knowing no one, and feeling like ducks out of water, their accidental meeting seemed fated. Mingling on the quad of the main campus they accidentally and literally bumped into each other. The first time they met apologies were extended, and each of them moved on. By the third such accidental meeting, after mutual "excuse-me's" and a host of "I'm so sorry(s)" were said, they looked at one another, broke into laughter and began conversing.

Being non-Indianans and new to the mid-west, they both had met only university officials, and some graduate students during the registration process. Their accidental encounters, and easy smiles fostered conversation, and a relationship was quick to develop. Finding the nearest cafeteria, they sat down over a cup of coffee to get to know each other better.

Rose Anne told Nan that she had come to *Purdue* because she had heard wonderful things about the university's College of Liberal Arts program in *American Studies*. It was program which integrated the creative arts into all of its graduate programs. On campus it was called the "Creative Initiative." The concept recently born locally, had gained national attention by being able to create a culture of creativity throughout the university.

Rose Anne shared that she had earned her Bachelor's and Master's degrees in Theater Arts, loved it, and knew that passion would be life-long. Yet by the time she had graduated she realized she wanted no part acting in the theater. She felt her main interests was in producing and directing, but really, was not totally sure. She was not comfortable on stage, but knew she needed some aspect of the theater to be part of her life. When she heard of Purdue's creative initiative, she became excited. Making numerous inquiries, and doing extensive research, she became convinced that Purdue would be the ideal place for her to study and to begin networking. The first week on campus convinced her she was absolutely correct as to her choice of schools, but without a car, with everything being so expensive and not yet being able to find affordable housing, she told Nan she was really starting to panic.

Nan said, "This is amazing! On a campus located in the heartland Indiana, miles from our home towns we meet each other, needing each other. I, as of yesterday, rented an apartment about one half hour from campus, on the outskirts of West Lafayette. It's too big for me, and I was hoping to be able to find a roommate. Bumping into you like this makes it seem that it is almost fated. This could be our lucky day, and I sure hope it is. If you have the time, we can take a drive to see the apartment. If it's to your liking, we can discuss how much your share of the rent would be, and if you like it, you could move in today." Rose Anne Tedico, sensing her prayers had been answered, sat back in her chair, and smiled the warmest smile she could remember smiling in years.

"Oh my God she said, this could be a miracle. If is okay with you, I have two appointments I must attend to, then I could meet you back here at 4:00 pm. Would that be okay?"

"4:00 pm it is!"

Although Rose Anne Tedico and Nan were total opposites in their life goals; Theater Arts and Technology, they hit it off like sugar and cream. Rose Anne was outgoing, effusive, approachable, Nan guarded, on the quiet-side and aggressive, yet they formed and immediate bond.

⁊

Rose Anne was from Nantucket Island in Massachusetts, just south of Cape Cod, an island with a relatively stable population of 5,600 folk, not counting the numerous, seasonal, affluent visitors.

She was an only child from a father who owned a small novelty and t-shirt store on Cape Cod, and a mother who sang in every amateur and stock opera /musical company that would have her.

As only child, Rose Anne had satisfied her mother's maternal instinct, but alas, never superseded her love for music. Her father adored her mother, but couldn't quite find the time, nor the manner, to invite his daughter into his emotions.

So Rose Anne, hence, grew up a "theater-brat," the stage as important in he education as her school. With her mother playing "the grand dame," Rose Anne was content to stay in the background, and by observing everything around her she learned the basics of putting a theater production together. A place she quickly adapted to and felt totally at home in. Yes, there was not much time for Mom's loving touch, but on the other hand it felt like home, safe and secure.

Nan, however, was the oldest of five girls, from a five acre farm on the outskirts of Eureka, Illinois, with a very busy, loving mother and an emotionally abusive father. It seemed the fates had truly stepped in when Rose Ann and Nan met.

Rose Anne, having spent most of her life in the background found comfort aiding others in reaching their potential. Her ego, satisfied by knowing she played a major role in another's success. Here at Purdue, the "Creative Initiative" concept was perfect for her. It allowed her to hone her skills by working with dynamic programs integrating her skills by forming consensus, and structuring viable wholes out of diverse entities.

Nan was driven to excel. Her need not only to succeed, but for recognition was driven by her need to be the very best, not only to succeed, but also to gain recognition. She realized it was in part driven by her need to prove to her father that she was worthy of his love. In reflective moments, she thanked God her personality was tempered by her mother's softness, love and gentility. She understood it was the influence of both her parents, that enabled her to become a rugged individualist, hell-bent on succeeding, balanced by an empathy and a tolerance for others.

The PhD program at Purdue gave Nan the intimacy of a small program, the personal attention, and at the same time it brought together some of the brightest minds pondering the potential of the impossible. Here she learned two lessons that would guide her for a life-time: never say never, and that inclusive is better than exclusive.

Both Nan and Rose Ann had created their own roadmap towards their future, and both were committed and persistent in pursuing it, yet each encouraged the other to be part of their different pathways of life, and participate when appropriate and possible. They learned from each other and for them it was the best of all worlds.

As the weeks turned into months, their friendship deepened. Before the year was out, without one modicum of effort they soon realized they became not only best friends, but lovers.

Book Four
Stewart Gill

May 20, 2007

Jefwin Apartments

3344 Arcane Avenue (a one bedroom apartment in a 25 year old complex, on a busy thorough-fare. (fifteen minutes from campus)

Stewart Gill, the oldest son of Hilda and Charles Gill didn't speak a word, didn't even babble until he was well into his third year on earth, although he did become fairly proficient in sign language. This was indicative of his capacity to learn.

Charles Gill, 37 years of age, Stewart's dad, worked at Danielle's Print Shop. A neighborhood print shop that has been around as long as anyone could remember. On the job Charles' responsibilities included cleaning the presses, stacking paper and monitoring ink supplies, keeping the shop clean, and on occasion, filling in on the guillotine-cutting machine when the other full-time employee was out sick. That didn't happen often, but when it did, the owner, Mr. Danielle was never more than a few feet from his side, making sure he didn't hurt himself, nor ruin a printed job. He had been working for Mr. Danielle for 20 years now, ever since graduating from St. Teresa's School for the Deaf, and felt very comfortable there. He basically did menial work, and shied away from any added responsibility. When factoring in the fact that most shop communication could be accomplished by pointing, his being deaf was not a problem.

Hilda Gill, Stewart's mom, had also been a student at St. Teresa's, started to go steady with Charles in the 11th grade. As it was. she and Charles both came from profoundly deaf parents, and were profoundly deaf themselves, so they blended together seamlessly. Having been sexually molested by a hearing, maintenance-man at St. Teresa's in the 7th grade, Hilda lived in a fearful world. It took four years for her to trust anyone to get close to her. Eventually, Charles with his charm and persistence was the first and only person since that rape to be able to get near her emotionally, and later touch her. His constant friendship, truthfulness, warmth and dependability eventually wore her defenses down, and they became boy and girlfriend. They lived together for a year without any problems, or major disagreements and both agreed the time was right for them to wed. Another factor, and perhaps more importantly, Hilda suspected she was pregnant.

They were married one year after graduating high school. The small wedding took place at the Deaf Club, the only social, and recreational environment in the area that people who were deaf felt comfortable attending. There were seven people in attendance: the bride and groom, the minister who was to perform the ceremony, the best man, Charles' only friend, the matron of honor, Hilda's only friend, and the Superintendent of the St. Teresa School for the Deaf and his wife.

Hilda's parents, who in the past couldn't wait for her to live away from home in the residence hall at St. Teresa's, informed their daughter they could not possibly attend the wedding because they lived ninety miles away and had no means of transportation to get them there. Charles' mother, and father had died in an automobile accident when he was twelve years old. Hilda and Charles didn't mind. They were most comfortable with each other, and the only people that they really liked and felt close to were in attendance.

The blissful couple rented a small two bedroom apartment on the top floor of a small apartment house, equi-distant from St. Teresa's, and Charles employer, Danielle's Print Shop. On the same block was a small grocery store in which one of the clerks knew finger spelling, so Hilda felt comfortable shopping there.

Within the year Stuart was born. One year and ten months later his sister, Veronica was born. Life was good for the Gill's. Charles was happy with his job, proud of his independence, his wife, home and his two children.

Hilda felt safe and comfortable. Her day was full taking care of, and playing with her two children, as well as running the household.

In spite of her contentment, Hilda did not venture too far from the Gill's apartment, not without Charles being at her side. Other than caring for her two children she had no other specific goals in life. Stewart was now four years old, and Veronica two years and one month. They filled her days and life. She needed nothing more.

Stewart, an intelligent child, picked up manual communication quite readily, as did his sister Veronica. Then one day in May his life changed. He came down with pneumonia.

His parents seeing his temperature soar to 104.7 began to panic, and rushed him to the emergency ward at the nearest hospital, where he was iced down, put on penicillin and immediately admitted to the hospital as an in-patient.

His parents were told, by writing notes back and forth, that he would be staying there for a few days until he was out of danger. Though concerned and fearful for their son, they didn't protest, for they were used to following the advice of hearing people.

The next day, an intern on his daily rounds, who just happened to have a deaf brother, saw Stewart signing to himself. Using sign language and voice, the intern approached Stewart and asked the boy where he learned sign language?

After a few seconds of scrutiny, Stewart responded by signing, "home". The doctor smiled, and continued on his rounds. Later that day he returned to the young boy's bed and again began to attempt to establish communication. At first, he pointed to himself, then signed and spoke, "my name is Dr. Rosen. What is your name?" An astonished Stewart simply stared back at the doctor. The doctor repeated, "My name is Dr. Rosen. What is your name?" This time Stewart signed his name, using the home-made sign his parents had taught him. The doctor, checking the chart at the side of his bed, pointed to his lips and said, "Stewart, your name is Stewart. Now watch my lips carefully and try to say Stew-art, Stew-art, Stew-art. After a little bit of coaxing, and a number of failed tries, Stewart began to utter, "Stew-art."

By the time Stewart was discharged, three days later, his spoken vocabulary had grown to roughly three dozen words. Dr.

Rosen, the intern convinced Stewart's parents it would not only be in Stewart's best interest, but also their own, to have Stewart learn spoken English. He suggested a pre-school program he knew of in the neighborhood that worked with bi-lingual children. Since it was sponsored by a local parish, it was free. If the parents agreed, the doctor would make some phone calls and see if there was a possibility of Stewart attending. They were thrilled to be able to communicate freely and easily, and after many questions agreed. There was an opening, and from that day forward Stewart Gill's life would not be the same.

The discovery that their child was not deaf had initially been traumatic for the Gills. How could they parent a hearing child? As he developed oral skills, how would they communicate? A thousand questions had raged through their minds, each question bringing more and more trepidation.

Actually the opposite occurred. As Stewart acquired more oral language, he become their bridge to the hearing world. With Stewart able to verbalize for her, Hilda Gill not only began to explore shopping beyond the local grocery store, but actually ventured forth, taking her children to the park on sunny days, and on long walks around the neighborhood. As long as Stewart was at her side, she felt more in control, calmer and in some strange way protected.

Soon the Gill's took young Stewart with them any time they went out. He gradually became the voice of the family. He had no real choice, especially after Dr. Rosen had his sister Veronica tested, and discovered she, like her parents, was also profoundly deaf.

Since his parents used no voice, and didn't possess a large English vocabulary, his responsibility to communicate and interpret his parents needs to the community-at-large weighed heavily on Stewart, until the day he left to attend college.

Life was not easy for the young boy. In school he was considered gifted, and excelled in all his classes. But to Stewart, "gifted" was an abstraction he could not internalize. He was driven to learn everything, for he felt the more knowledge he acquired, the better he would be able to cope with and do for his family.

By the time he was in the fifth grade, he had assumed most of the verbal and societal responsibilities for his family's household. But like many other children of deaf adults (CODA), he suffered miserably in silence, although not always passively. The fact that he was such a good student and always polite with adults, saved him a number of times from being thrown out of school for fighting. He had no friends, not because he didn't want friends, he simply had no time for them. After school he would hurry home, knowing he would be needed by his mother to either interpret for her, escort her, or do something similar for the other members of his family.

Without any kind of interaction with others of his own age, Stewart's social skills were at best awkward, and he found it very difficult to relate age-appropriately with his classmates. Since he excelled in all subjects, from Art, especially Art to Math, from History to English, from Geography to Science, his peers could only taunt him about his parents and sister being deaf, and how he was such a "Nerd!" Behind his back, his class mates would produce funny sounds, mimicking the occasional sounds one or two of them had heard deaf people make when verbalizing, exercising more patience than most young children have, he would try to ignore them, but eventually their jealousies and cruelties would get under his skin. And because he also excelled in boxing and better yet, fighting, he would finally respond with his fists.

Since Stewart was of average height and weight for a fifth grader, the bigger kids in school thought he would be a push-over and initially went out of their way to tease and make fun of him. Stewart's response was as vicious as it was swift. As soon as a taunt began, he would punch, kick, scratch with such a vengeance that it took a teacher, and sometimes two, to end the brawl.

After the third fight of the academic year, Stewart's mother was asked to attend a meeting in the Assistant Principal's office. At first she refused, frightened and uncomfortable at the thought of being with hearing people. But when Stewart explained he would be thrown out of school if she didn't attend the meeting, she knew she had no choice. Stewart convinced her not to worry, because he would get permission to leave school and escort her from home to the Assistant Principal's office, and back home again. Not only would he be with her at all times, but would interpret for her. Only then did she reluctantly agree to come.

In attendance at the meeting was the Assistant Principal, Stewart's class-room teacher, the school counselor, a secretary who would record the events of the meeting, and finally, Stewart and his mother.

The meeting began with the Assistant Principal pontificating about the school being a place of learning, and how violence in any form could not and would not be tolerated. Even though Stewart interpreted word-for-word what was being said, he intuitively understood that his mother was not internalizing anything. Watching her close to tears, sitting with her hands tightly clasped on her knees, her eyes unblinking, and her body absolutely still, Stewart found himself vacillating between anger and pity. Couldn't they, anyone in that room, see his mother's pain? These people were supposed to be educators, couldn't they understand that his mother was overwhelmed and frightened?

What was wrong with them?" His mother did not ask a single question, and only nodded her head a few times when she felt all eyes were looking at her.

Stewart was signing as clearly and quickly as he could. His hands and wrists were tired when the Assistant Principal summed up the meeting by saying, "even though young Stewart was defending the honor of his family, and was a very good student, the violence had to end.

These incidents had not been merely scraps between two young boys. Stewart had sent one boy to the hospital, and drawn blood from two others. Since the school seemed unable to convince Stewart his behavior was unacceptable, it would now be up to Mr. and Mrs. Gill to find a way to put some sense in the boy's head, if not, he would be suspended."

That evening was one of the toughest times of Stewart's life. The atmosphere at dinner was excruciatingly painful. Even his little sister sensed something was afoot. With dinner served, Stewart and Veronica cleared the table and began to do the dishes while his mother tried to explain to his father what had occurred earlier that afternoon. What she communicated in sign, pointing to Stewart was, "fight, bad, could suspend from school." When his father turned towards him and asked him to explain more, Stewart felt stuck. How could he tell his parents people were making fun of them and his sister? How could he explain his feeling of alienation?

He couldn't.

So he promised his parents he would not get into any more fights in school, a promise he kept by imploding not exploding. A personality trait established by circumstance, and that would serve him well in his career, but cause him havoc in his personal life.

Upon entering Junior High School, Stewart encountered a Physical Education teacher who would not only change his life, but establish a path for his future.

Nathan Peters, orphaned at the age of six, was raised by an aunt and uncle who happened to be deaf. Having lived through many of the experiences young Stewart was going through now, he recognized Stewart was a boy in need, and thought about how he might be able to mentor him. After looking at Stewart's academic record, he realized here was a young man who possessed all the tools needed to make a difference in this world He saw much of himself in Stewart, and resolutely decided he would do what he could to help this young man reach his full potential.

Having made the decision to mentor the boy, he sat back on his chair and began to wonder if this was the reason he had learned specific lessons in life; about deafness, love and responsibility? Wasn't this why he was able to understand this particular young man? Interesting, he thought.

Coach Peters had noticed Stewart the first week of class. Having played varsity basketball at Long Island University and loving the game with a passion, the coach used basketball as an evaluative tool to get a handle of the athletic skills of his students. Since there were four baskets in the gym, he had separated his thirty-two students into eight teams of four, and had them play four-on-four, half court basketball.

In this manner, it didn't take long to adjust the competition, pairing those who could play the game with others who could play the game, and those who played at the game with students with similar abilities. It was during this process that he noticed Stewart stood out from the rest.

Even though the boys in his group were taller, faster and leaner, Stewart seemed to have the natural ability to excel in every facet of the game. Under the basket Stewart knew where to position himself; how to use his body to block out, and out-rebound the taller boys. As a shooter, he was efficient and graceful, but it was his overall feel for the game, that as a seventh grader was a rarity. Most kids his age were only interested in shooting the ball. Combining unselfishness on the court, with his athletic prowess, Mr. Peters could see this boy was special. Yet he noticed Stewart seemed to be a loner. He shared no camaraderie with his fellow students; when he wasn't in a specific activity, he was standing alone. There was something about the boy that seemed to remind him of himself.

"Gil! After class come see me."

"Can't, got other classes."

"Okay, after school come see me in my office."

"Can't, gotta go home, have family responsibilities."

"Be there! I'll write you a note."

"Can't, my parents are deaf, and my mother needs me at home to interpret."

"I understand, I was raised by an aunt and uncle who where deaf."

"You sign?"

"Of course I sign, I told you I was raised by deaf relatives. You be sure to be there in my office after school. I'll wait."

Stewart showed up at Mr. Peters' office.

"I've looked at your academic record, and must say it was one of the more interesting records I have seen in a long time. Got into any fights lately?"

"No, no, I haven't! They told me I would be expelled from school if I got into another fight. That's why I stay away from the other kids. They like to tease, and pull my chain, and I get angry, so it's easier just to hang-out by myself."

"Okay, I understand. Tell you why I asked you to see me. I work at the settlement house down the street three afternoons after school, and three evenings a week. I'm forming a basketball league, and I could use your help. You have a good command of the game, and on the court you are a natural leader. I think you would enjoy yourself, and no one would dare make fun of you when you are working for me. Granted it doesn't pay much, seventy-five cents an hour, but for the ten hours a week, you'll have some spending money. What do you say?"

"Mr. Peters, it sounds good, but like I told you before, I got family responsibility. So thanks, but no thanks." Stewart got up to leave, but Mr. Peters was not through.

"I'll tell you what I will do. Let me speak to your parents directly. I'm sure something can be worked out."

"I don't know. My parents aren't comfortable with hearing people. The last time my mother was with hearing people was when I got into a fight in school, and she was asked to come to the principle's office to hear some crap about me. She was so scared that even though I interpreted every word they said, she didn't understand anything. She just sat there petrified, and those bastards didn't do anything to make her feel at ease. Every time I tried to explain something to them, they told me to be seen and not heard and to do nothing but interpret. When I started getting upset, my mother began to cry. I promised her I would not cause trouble and she calmed down after that. When the meeting was over, I ignored the assholes, put my arm around my mom's waist, and we walked all the way home.

My dad works at Danielle's Print Shop, and is one of two employees. You know something? Even though he's been working there for more than twenty years, his boss and the guy he works with have never bothered to learn even one word of sign language. He tells me that when he doesn't understand what they are saying to him, they just talk louder. You want to talk stupid, that to me Mr. Peters is just plain damn ignorant! The only friends my parents have are some deaf people, and they meet with them a couple of times a month at the deaf club. Other than that, they are just not comfortable going out anywhere unless I am there with them. So you see, it just wouldn't work out."

Listening to the boy talk, almost brought tears to Peters eyes. He recalled the number of times he had to intervene for his aunt and uncle. How they would not do anything without him. But they had a farm, and for the most part were self-sufficient. They had some speech training, and if they really tried hard, could make themselves understood. So he had time to play ball and participate in a variety of activities. This exposure had helped his personal and academic life immensely.

"I'll tell you what. You ask them if it will be okay for me to stop by Thursday evening after dinner. Tell them I am only asking for ten minutes of their time. And I don't need an interpreter."

It was only a ten minute walk from the settlement house to the Gill's residence. The only element that distinguished the house they lived in from the hundreds of similar houses around them, was a small light that had been installed next to a buzzer, just under the mail box which had their name on it. When the buzzer was pushed outside a similar light which was installed next to the buzzer in their kitchen blinked. In that manner, the Gil's knew when someone was downstairs. By pushing the buzzer in the kitchen, the buzzer under the mailbox blinked as well, telling the guest someone was home.

Seeing the blinking light, Peters knew the Gill family was waiting for him. With the gait of an athlete, he ascended the stairs, and knocked on their door. Stewart opened it, and with a nervous smile asked him to come in. He entered into the kitchen and without prompting signed and spoke, "Good to see you Stewart." As he completed the sentence he thrust his hand out to Stewart as a sign of greeting. Stewart shook his hand, and led him to the kitchen table where his mom, dad and sister were seated.

Realizing using voice was a waste, he began to sign to the family. "Thank you for seeing me. My name is Nathan Peters, and I am Stewart's gym teacher at William J. Gaynor Junior High School. The reason I am here tonight is, I also work three days a week at the Williamsburg Settlement House. The settlement house offers a variety of programs to young people in this area. It's open after school five days a week and on Saturdays. The entire facility and all programs are free to all neighborhood children. I am in charge of all the athletic programs at the settlement house. Your son is a gifted athlete, excelling in basketball, and for that reason I would like Stewart to work for me as my assistant, eight hours a week after school, two hours on Monday, and three hours on Wednesday and Friday."

When Mr. Peters stopped signing, Stewart's parents looked at one another cautiously, then at Stewart, then back at each other then signed to Mr. Peters, "Are you deaf?"

"No."

"Then where did you learn to sign?"

The gym teacher smiled to himself knowing it was more important to them the way he signed, than what he signed. He knew his sign language was as fluid as a native deaf person, and that, more than any other factor would convince Stewart's parents to trust him. He was right. After a little more than five minutes of general conversation, the Gill's gave their permission for Stewart to work for Nathan Peters.

On the following Monday, after school, on the basketball court of the Williamsburg Settlement House, a teacher was born. A teacher who would make a big difference in the lives of many young people.

Big brother, uncle, surrogate father, coach, no matter what it was called, the relationship between the Nathan Peters and Stewart Gill became as tight as a relationship could become. The Gill's were thrilled their son not only had someone he could talk with, but more importantly, had a hearing adult, trustworthy, who could guide their son, in a way they were not able to.

The teacher, not a especially gregarious man, not a highly sociable man, a man with very little family to speak of, found in Stewart Gill a *younger* brother he could mentor, share with, and in general, fill some void in his personal life.

Stewart Gill felt like a child reborn. The vast burden he had felt having to cater to his parents, being the sole link between his parents and the hearing world seemed lifted. He now had a job that would earn him money, cash he would no longer have to depend upon his parents for. Though they always gave him an allowance, he knew his Dad didn't earn much, now he could turn to his mom and tell her to use the money to buy something nice for herself. That made him feel good. Now he also had a *teacher, big brother, coach, friend* who was, more times than not, bossy, demanding and tough, but at the same time always fair, honest and up-front with him. Truth was, he had become his only friend.

꩜

May 20, 2007

Jefwin Apartments

"Funny how one's life goes."

He thought to himself that his coming down with pneumonia as a child, and playing basketball in junior high school had changed his life.

Dr. Rosen and Coach Peters were never really far apart from him, And even though he had not seen those two men in years, he carried them with him in his heart. Even now, before responding to a situation, he would ask himself, "what would Coach do?"

He loved his parents, but never felt he could go to them for counsel, or assistance. "They are good people, but ..."

It was awfully lonesome growing up feeling isolated from everyone, feeling so all alone..

He hated getting all dressed up. Growing up in a family without a lot of money to spend on clothing, had limited his wardrobe as a child and as a young man. He could not help but smiling to himself over his use of the term wardrobe. All items were bought a size larger (room to grow into, he was told), in a material that would not wear out, and pretty much anything that was on sale.

Clothing therefore had never meant anything special to him,. Oh yes, he understood the concept of color theory, probably more than most. He could use color effectively in designing a piece of graphics, or creating an illustration, but he seemed to be color blind when choosing something to wear. That was why, in recent years, he would only buy apparel in either black or gray. This way he could dress in the dark, which he did often, wasting no time wondering if his choice of separates matched, and also he could be pretty sure he would still look okay; then he smiled to himself, rationalizing *style* was a personal choice.

He remembered teasing Coach for the haphazard way he dressed, yet it never dawned on him that he was equally blind to what he wore. To both, there were more important things in life than what you had on your back. He mused to himself, well I'm *never* going to change. To change you need to *want* to change, and I guess, no I *know,* I do not *want* to change. I will *never* change, that's *me.*

Armed with that knowledge, he now patted himself on his back, pleased in knowing that he had been wise enough to have bought a suit he could wear on any occasion, his *one* black suit.

"Black is good. Black is beautiful. Black never goes out of style. I sure hope so, cause if it does, I'm in deep shit. But for now, everything is cool. I will don the white shirt I bought last month, and my favorite grey tie. No one has to know it is my one and only tie, consequently, it is my favorite."

Man, Gill… you will look like a real cool dude."

Having showered and shaved, he donned his "dress uniform" and looked at himself in the mirror, something he chose not do often. He almost didn't recognize the image looking back at him from the mirror. "Not bad, he said to himself, in fact you look pretty damn good!"

Thinking about his presentation for the big night, he couldn't help but recall how far, wide and circuitous his journey to this day had been. The movie in his mind began to play backwards, and stopped when he found himself in Coach Peters office midway through eighth grade. He remembered that moment as if it was yesterday.

There was the Coach, from out of the blue, telling him that he had made an appointment for him to show his portfolio to the admissions person at *the School for the Arts* two weeks hence.

Allowing some time for the information to sink in, he then attempted to explain to Stewart why he did what he did.

The School for the Arts was in his opinion not only unique, but considered by many, one of the best in the city school system. It was only large enough to accommodate three hundred and twenty students, and only accepted sixty students a year. So if you were accepted, you knew they thought you had talent.

The Coach realized it was located more than an hour away from home, but from everything he had heard it was more than worth it. Yes, he would have to travel by bus and by train, but for the opportunity, a small price to pay. Sure, it would be a long day when you totaled the almost three hours a day traveling to and from the school, the eight hours a day of classes. Four hours were spent studying art, four hours studying various academic subjects, and one hour for lunch. It made for a very long day, but Coach believed it was well worth it. No-where else could he get this high quality education in both art and academics. Coach further explained that eighty-five per cent of the *School of the*

Arts graduates, went on to college, and the other fifteen per cent found jobs in the areas they studied. He said the *School for the Arts* was considered one of the best of the schools in the entire city. And since Stewart trusted the Coach's judgment, he should take his advise.

In ending his speech to Stewart, he added that he just happened to be friends with Coach Sandler, the athletic director of the school and its basketball coach, and predicted to him that Stewart would star on the junior varsity team his first year, and be starting guard on the varsity by tenth grade.

Then he said he expected Stewart would go on the interview, and show his portfolio. The "**you will**" always got Stewart's attention, but the final decision to go or not to go would be up to Stewart. He planned to stop up and see Stewart's parents, explain his recommendations, and address any concerns they might have. His monologue ended with, "Gill, you have nothing to lose, and possibly a lot to gain."

Stewart's portfolio consisted of twelve drawings: three in (color) pencil, three in pen and ink and six black and white pencil drawings. Not a lot, but each of the drawings had received an "A" from his teacher, with the comment, "excellent work!" Along with the drawings, he had a letter of introduction from Coach Peters, a copy of his transcript, and a letter of recommendation from his art teacher.

In the Spring when Stewart got the letter of acceptance, Coach insisted on visiting his parents again, only this time he brought with him a bottle of sparkling wine. He said it was to be a celebration of Stewart's achievement, and a celebration of his parent's excellent and loving parenting.

Coach later explained to Stewart his reasons. Trying never to miss an opportunity to teach his "ward" something of import. By bringing Stewart's parents into the process, and eliminating all doubt that the decision was a good one, reinforced the decision as meritorious, and at the same time created an atmosphere of participation and unity.

This was a technique he had learned in graduate school, a technique called, *future pacing.*

Thinking back to that evening he recalled how eloquent and fluid Coach's signing was. His body language, his expressions, his clarity. It was also a joy to see his parents so comfortable and almost smug, full of pride, and sipping the sparkling wine the Coach had poured for them.

Stewart felt real good knowing he was responsible for his parent's joy.

Coach completed his presentation by adding the fact that there was one deaf student already enrolled in the school, and to support him the school had purchased a TTY; which he mentioned, would afford Mr. and Mrs. Gill, Stewart and the school a method of communication.

Coach was very persuasive and by the end of the evening Stewart knew he would be attending the School for the Arts.

Now as the movie in his mind was playing in fast forward, his high school years went flying by, stopping only at the time he was suspended for hitting a teacher. To this day he believed he was justified.

The teacher was not really a teacher, but a professional artist the school had hired as Adjunct, to teach a class in *Sign and Showcard*, otherwise known as hand-lettering.

In this class students were expected to master specific brush lettering skills. Being a southpaw, lettering from left to right with wet paint, and at the same time, a different kind of learner, now known by the term, *dyslexia*, Stewart found it necessary to find his own way to accomplish a task. In the past, as long as he performed that task at a high level, he was given the latitude to deviate from a set of procedures that he was not comfortable with.

That son-of-a-bitch, the teacher, what-ever-his-name was disagreed. He came by Stewart's desk, watched him work for a moment, then reached down grabbed the paper, ripped it into pieces; then threw the debris at Stewart saying, "you will do the assignment my way, or no way! Do you understand?"

Stewart's response was at first confusion, then surprise. As he noticed everyone in the class looking at him and laughing, his temper got the best of him, and he uttered. more to himself than out-loud, "fuck you mister." It was the most clever remark he could think of at the moment.

At first his teacher could not believe he heard what he thought he heard. Backing away, the look on his face changed from puzzlement to a sadistic smirk. He ordered Stewart to stand up and repeat what he had said.

With clarity of voice, not moving an inch, looking right at the teacher, Stewart did.

"Get up Gill, now!"

As he began to rise from his seat, without warning, the teacher slapped him across his face.

Without thinking of the ramifications, Stewart remembered nailing that cocksucker with a left hand punch, which began as far down as his knee, and made contact with the teacher's jaw in one beautiful arc. The man went down like a tub of shit, and Stewart, not knowing what else to do walked out of the class. Later that day he was informed that he had been suspended from classes, and that the what's-his-name was planning not only to bring charges against him, but to have him arrested as well.

Thank you Coach Peters… I don't know where I would have been if you hadn't come into my life."

He remembered how Coach interceded for him once again. He'd made phone calls, spoke to some students, and faculty and found out the facts, and then convinced what-ever-his- name was that it would be in his best interest to simply forget the entire episode.

He did.

It was later agreed that the teacher would not be coming back to teach at the school, and Stewart would be allowed to go back to classes.

That evening in the Settlement House Coach Peters chewed Stewart's ass out in the privacy of his office, like it had never been chewed out before, or since.

He pointed out to him in a very cogent manner that the major flaw in his personality, was his temper. Now that he was closing in on adulthood, fighting was no longer a viable solution. Fighting was something kids did in the neighborhood to prove how macho they were. Fighting was never an answer, and never would be. He told Stewart that as an adult, every time you use your fists and not your brain, you are risking a potential felony offense, possibly punishable by jail time. He then reminded Stewart, once again, at a decibel level his mother and father could hear, in language so simple and direct it could not be confused, of his responsibility to his parents, his school, his teammates and to himself. Before kicking Stewart out of his office he added that if he ever felt the need to use his fists again, Coach would be happy to accommodate him, and promised he would not hold anything back. Whether it was fear, or common sense that registered that evening, Stewart Gill never got into another fight.

A-mental-fast forward again to his senior year

Removing a cold *Corona* from his refrigerator, he pulled open the tab as he slumped down on his couch. Yes, his senior year had been memorable. He was the first *School of the Arts* athlete to be awarded with the distinction of "All State."

Remembering the number of colleges that had expressed enough interest in him to offer him a four year scholarship for his basketball talents, still made him feel good. After weighing each offer and opportunity with Coach Sandler and Coach Peters, he reduced the list to two schools, The *University of Illinois*, and *the University of California at Los Angeles, U.C.L.A.* Both had outstanding basketball programs as well as excellent schools of Art.

His parents as he had expected wanted him to stay closer to home and attend The *University of Illinois.* They told him they would miss him terribly; that his sister needed a big brother, and finally, truthfully asked, "who will interpret for us when we need it?"

They had argued that the *University of Illinois* offered everything he had said he wanted. On top of that, their friends at the deaf club told them the *University of Illinois* had a very good reputation, and *Big Ten* basketball, whatever that was, was as good as anything he could find out west.

He remembered clearly his suppressed anger, and the silent discussion he had with himself. "How the hell would they know what I want or need. They never attended a game, never even seen me play in practice. I doubt they even know the difference between a basketball and a football."

These thoughts he had kept to myself.

When they were finished, Stewart countered their arguments with…

He had grown to really detest winters in Chicago. He was tired of the severe weather of the Midwest. Freezing rain blowing in from the lake, tons of snow in the winter and hot-as-hell in the summer. *U.C.L.A.* on the other hand, offered great weather, had a great school of Art, and also one of the most respected basketball programs in the country. As for his sister, Veronica, he told them that she reminds him, almost on a daily basis, to mind his own business, that she is old enough to make her own decisions, and this big brother crap doesn't fly. And lastly, talking about his little sister, she had developed sufficient oral skills to be able to intercede for his parents when necessary.

What he didn't, couldn't say, because he loved them… was he believed this was one of the only opportunities he would ever have to break free.

He knew that the only way he would get to find out what he was capable of, and who he was, was to get away.

He remembered his mother starting to cry, and his father putting his arm around her shoulders, turning to his son and signing, "then you have to do what you have to do."

It seemed the older he became, the wider the polarities of his emotions. He was either happy and immersed in his studies, or he was filled with an anger he didn't understand.

His parents and sister had never seen him play one minute of basketball. He recalled how hurt he had felt back then. Lamenting out loud he said, "I was good. I was captain of the team, I made all-state, and was written up in newspapers often. I was acknowledged as an outstanding scholar/athlete, was invited along with my parents to numerous dinners, which of course I didn't go to, because I didn't want to be the only student there without his parents. I saw my teammates parents watching them practice, waiting after school for them, cheering and rooting for them, but never once, were my parents there to share my moments of success or to encourage me."

He recalled the intensity of his anger and anguish, and knew he could not stop it. He had to leave before he said anything or did something he couldn't take back, and would regret later, rationalizing the best thing he could do for his family and for himself, was go far away.

He knew it was the right decision to go west, but he still felt guilty remembering his mother's tears. He was spending more time in the gym, at school and at the Settlement House, anywhere but home. Soon he would be heading west.

It couldn't happen soon enough.

It was Coach Peters, who, on a windy day towards the end of August drove Stewart to the airport. In the discussions they had in the last few months, young Gill had bared many of his feelings. Coach had listened quietly, nodding his head in understanding, and stated that he knew *his kid-brother, his protégée* needed to get away and go west.

What Stewart remembered most of those discussions was that before each time he left the coach's office, he would tell Stewart how proud he was of him, and that whatever the future had in store for him, wherever the winds would take him, that he would always be proud of him.

The Coach didn't say much on the journey to *O'Hare Airport*, although Stewart did notice him watching him out of the corner of his eye, and smiling. They pulled up to the terminal building of *American Airlines*, and Coach helped him gather his luggage. It was then he saw a tear in his couch's eye, and heard a deep sadness in his voice when he said "I'll miss you boy. Good luck and good bye."

May 20, 2007

Jefwin Apartments

"Where did the years go ?"

He looked around at his apartment, noticing for the first time how spartan his environment now looked. All the possessions, the trappings of his past were no longer part of his world. When, and where did they go?

He hadn't smoked a single cigarette that day. He was proud of his ability to cut his smoking habit by more than half when he chose to do so, but today he rationalized he was entitled to indulge. As he lit up, his thoughts again returned to his past. Growing up he didn't have much, and didn't need much. As he got older *things* began to represent success. Acquiring *things* felt good, and it was important for to him to feel good.

U.C.L.A. had not worked out in the manner he had expected.

The College of Art was wonderful. His drawing and design skills improved and were finely honed. The classes he took in the history of Art helped him understand what was happening in the Art world today, and became the foundation for the work he would do in the future.. He realized Art was not just something people did for fun, but Art was profound. Art made people feel good. Art was not only a recorder of history, but an antennae for life as well.

It was during these four years that he had matured into a serious artist, became a hard working adult.

But the events that did most to make him into the person he was, were his basketball experiences.

Being recruited by one of the top basketball programs in the country, having made all-state in his senior year, being named the most valuable player by his teammates that same year of high school, had made him feel real good about who he was. He walked tall knowing everyone in school knew him.

He recalled how this image of himself began to change the first day of basketball practice. Even before he had put his uniform on, he knew things would not be the same as it was in high school. At 5' 8 ½" he was the shortest man on the team. In high school he had faced one or two tall players, here they all were tall. Not only were they taller, but as he later discovered they were faster, quicker and stronger.

At *U.C.L.A.*, coming out for basketball practice didn't always mean you would be playing basketball. Before the season began, basketball practice was body conditioning. The program began by running, moved on to more running, then to even more running. When the players were not running up and down the court, or running the outdoor or indoor track, they were running the steps in the gym. This was interspersed with working out in the weight room, where one of the coaches would determine the amount of weight each player would work out with. Once that was decided, the assistants would assign a specific program and determine the number of repartitions.

This team would not lose a game because any student was out of shape.

In the conditioning room and on the track, Stewart was able to hold his own by sheer determination, and at times even out-do his fellow teammates. It was on the basketball court that the vast difference in talent showed. Not that he was bad, he was good and he knew it, but these guys were simply superb athletes.

Nevertheless, when on the court he fought for every ball and gave one hundred and ten percent of everything he had in him.

The coach would smile at his willingness to push himself so relentlessly, and for his discipline in learning and running the set-play offenses. His teammates in a short while also began to respect him for his tenacity and toughness.

But in big-time college basketball, tenacity and toughness are not enough. Talent, height, and the ability to put the basketball through the hoop is what is important. Though he ran the offense as well as the three other point guards on the team, when it came to rebounding, shooting and defense, he paled by comparison to them. For his entire basketball career at *U.C.L.A.* he was relegated to be part of the mop-up squad who played only at the end of games that couldn't be won or lost.

To his credit, he never complained. In his Art classes he was a star. On the basketball court, he wasn't.

The lessons he learned those days were going to pay off "big-time" in his future.

He completed his Bachelor of Fine Arts degree in four years, completed the Master of Fine Arts degree in another two, and because the chairman of the department had taken a liking to him, he was hired to teach drawing and painting upon his graduation. Within three years he was promoted from Lecturer to Instructor, and from Instructor to Assistant Professor.

Life was good, the pay wasn't, but at this juncture in his life it didn't matter.

May 20, 2007

Jefwin Apartments

"Well, I can't say it hasn't been an interesting journey."

All this nostalgia was getting to him. Beer, even good Mexican beer was not doing the job. He got up, went to the cabinet above his sink in the kitchen part of his studio apartment. Took down a bottle of scotch, and poured himself a drink. Fortified with his scotch companion, he returned to his favorite chair, and returned to his memories.

He thought back to that Spring evening when he went to the Cinema Theater, right in the heart of Westward, less than a mile from his apartment, "*Love is a many splendid thing*" was playing. It just happened to be one of his favorite movies, and Jennifer Jones was one of his favorite actresses. He had developed a crush on her from the first time he saw her. She represented everything he believed beauty to be.

The question… Why did he, in the middle of the week, do something he never did, go to the movies?

"Is everything preordained?

Are we just acting out a script that was written?" Questions he thought about quite often.

The movie was just as good the third time he saw it. But when exiting the theater a certain sadness entered his being. He felt enveloped by a cloak of loneliness. He realized he was so caught up in his teaching, and working on a new series of paintings, that he had not allowed himself time to admit to himself that he was lonely. It hit him like a ton of bricks. He had not been on a date, nor been to a party in more than half a year, six months, holy shit six months!

He admitted to himself that he was not a joiner, nor very gregarious. And yes, he was basically alone when not in the classroom, but six months… ?

Though he had never considered himself a *Romeo*, at the same time, he wasn't ugly. He enjoyed the company of women when he had the time, and thought they enjoyed being with him. But six months? He began to feel regret for the opportunities he passed over for one reason or another.

In the middle of his internal dialogue, he spotted a new restaurant/bar that wasn't there the last time he was in this area. *Alice's Restaurant.* He loved the movie, Arthur Penn was a superb director, and Arlo Guthrie's *Alice's Restaurant's Massacre* was one of his favorite songs.

He thought, "what the hell, I don't feel like going home yet. One drink won't kill me."

He entered the restaurant, and immediately began analyzing the décor.

"Not quite diner-like, nevertheless, homey. Probably a franchise, or a franchise to-be."

Since this was a weekday, and late in the evening the place was not crowded, in fact the bar was empty, save for a very pretty bartender. As he approached the bar, she nodded to him and smiled. "Hi Professor Gill, how you doing? What can I get for you?"

Taken back, he looked intensely at her trying to ascertain how she knew him. She did look a little familiar, but that was it.

"Don't remember me, do you? That makes me sad. I'll bet you dollar to donuts I know the reason you don't remember me. Yep, you don't remember me because I have my clothes on. I modeled for your figure drawing class earlier this year. If you'd like, if itwould help, I'll get undressed."

He smiled. "That won't be necessary. I do remember you, Judith right? I don't remember your last name, but I do remember you correcting me when I called you Judy. You said, not even my parents call me Judy, my name is Judith."

She chuckled, recalling the incident.

"Was that the reason I didn't get a call-back? Did you feel chagrined that a mere model was correcting you, or was it the fact that you just didn't like my body?"

"No, no, that was not the reason, though at this point in time I don't recall what the reason was. Nevertheless I do remember saying to myself, yes, that woman has a beautiful body."

From that chance meeting at Alice's Restaurant, a romance blossomed.

Before he left that evening the figure model and the teacher set a date for lunch that upcoming Saturday. He suggested they meet at a lovely bar called *Monte's* in Santa Monica, right on the ocean, two miles east of Wilshire Boulevard. She knew the place and thought it was a wonderful suggestion.

They hit it off. Boy, did they hit it off. Within a month they were seeing each other on a steady basis. Within one week after agreeing they would not be seeing anyone else, they were sleeping together. And within three months, they were seriously talking about getting married. Fourteen weeks after they met at *Alice's Restaurant*, they flew off for a weekend to Reno and got married.

Judith Barrington Gill, nee Judith Barrington Silver, Stewart Gill's newly acquired wife was quite a package. Oh, he recalled she was more than a package, she was a package and a half. Within the first month of marriage, he discovered that his testosterone could not keep up with her hormones. He doubted there was enough testosterone in the world to keep up with his new wife. The more he gave, the more she wanted. Stewart was finding it close to impossible to keep up with his beautiful wife.

A while back, while teaching a figure drawing class, recruiters from Disney came into the class to observe. He was demonstrating 30 second gesture drawing, while giving a running dialogue on the importance of seeing, not just looking, but really seeing, then transferring those images to whatever surface you were working on, with whatever tool you were using.

After class one of the recruiters approached him, commenting on his amazing drawing skills, and mentioned that Disney was always looking for talent like his. If he was ever interested on becoming an animator, a job would be his for the asking. Then she threw in, "and let me tell you, the pay and the benefits are pretty darn good.

As his body began wearing down, he came to the realization that his wife was insatiable in the bedroom. At the same time he also realized her ability to spend money was equal to her sexual prowess, and… out-equaled his ability to earn. He had half a problem most men he knew said they would die for, and half a problem most men feared.

What was he going to do? Rationalizing, he figured her sexual appetite would abate in time, but there was no way he could keep up with her taste on a teacher's salary.

It was then he recalled the conversation he had with the recruiter from Disney Studios. He decided to call.

"What was her name, come on fella, you can remember. Yes, yes that's it, Elizabeth Baldwin."

He called.

Yes she did remember him, how could she forget someone with his skills. And yes the offer was still good. And… when would he be coming out to Disney Studio to see her.

Two weeks later, he drove out to Burbank. After an initial interview with Elizabeth (call her Liz) Baldwin, she introduced him to a gentleman by the name of George Hanna, who worked in the animation department. George as he asked Stewart to call him, explained everyone involved in animation at Disney was as easy-going as they were creative. It was he who took him on a tour of the facilities. "Impressive" doesn't begin to describe how Stewart felt about what he was experiencing. George then brought him to a room on the ground floor where a drawing class was in session. He explained that at Disney, nothing was more important than drawing skills, and maintenance of those skills. That was why all the animators on staff were encouraged to attend as many of the drawing classes as possible.

Upon entering the room, Stewart could not believe what he was seeing. There before his eyes was a blocked-off area containing, two cows, four pigs, a half dozen ducks, an equal amount of chickens, and three goats.

George explained that a short film based on the song *Old MacDonald Had a Farm*, starring the inimitable *Donald Duck* was just beginning its initial stages of production. To foster familiarity, and enable the animation staff to be more facile with the drawing of the farm animals in the film, it was easier to have the animals brought to the studio, then to have the animators travel to a farm.

And so, the animation staff was encouraged to draw, draw and draw some more.

Stewart was asked if he would like to try his hand. A quick, "you betcha," got him an 18"x24" newsprint drawing pad, some drawing pencils, charcoal, conte crayons, and a light easel. Removing his jacket, rolling up his sleeves he literally attacked the drawing surface, in doing so, demonstrated prodigious skills.

It did not take the animators in attendance long to recognize Stewart's drawing skills were outstanding. As a unit they agreed he would be an asset to their department. He was escorted him back to Elizabeth Baldwin's office by another animator, said his name was Eric, since George, his initial guide was caught up sketching. After some polite chatter Elizabeth Baldwin made him an offer that was double his current salary. An offer he just couldn't turn down.

His Department Chairperson, Dr. Engers, the same person who had originally hired him, was not happy with the news that he would be leaving especially before the end of the semester. No matter what he said, Gill had his mind made up. Not being able to talk some sense into his head, he begrudgingly accepted the fact that Professor Stewart Gill, a wonderful young teacher, a natural in the classroom, would be leaving.

※

The next five months were exciting. He was learning the Disney system for making animation, drawing eight to ten hours a day, and loving every minute of it. In fact he welcomed the alarm clock going off in the morning. Most days he was wide-awake before it even went off. A shower, morning coffee, a hug and a kiss from his beautiful wife (one time he made the mistake of a second kiss, and missed the day's work), and off to a pleasant drive to Burbank, thinking, life was good, life was very, very good.

It didn't take long for the loving couple to move into a brand-new large apartment, and begin the process of furnishing it.

Alas, the fun soon wore off when he rediscovered his wife, along with good taste, had a real talent to spend money. A talent that dwarfed her beauty.

All his attempts to reel in her buying sprees were useless. She was spending money faster than he was able to earn it. Factoring into the equation that keeping his wife happy at nights, and weekends, and putting in ten hour days at work was wearing him down.

Nevertheless, he was a trouper, and he knew somehow he would find a solution. He was not a quitter, and would do his best to make this marriage work.

Burning the candle at both ends soon became untenable. He was becoming too tired to produce in the bedroom, starting to lose his focus at work, and to his wife's chagrin, had the audacity to criticize her spending habits.

It was not surprising the relationship soon turned sour.

Within days of their first "good old fashioned" spat about money, she began to stay out all night. Within weeks, days became weekends, and when he confronted her wanting to know where she was, and what was going on, she told him she was out looking for a real man, and the rest of what she was doing was none of his fucking business.

Before long, the only thing they agreed on was that this marriage was doomed to failure.

The next weekend they flew to Reno, where less than a year before they entered into wedded bliss, now they were going for a blissful divorce.

Though he loved drawing, he began to hate animation. The rules of simplification and exactitude were driving him crazy. He began dreaming of his life "pre" Judith Barrington Gill, nee Judith Barrington Silver, the old days of drawing a figure, a face as he saw it, or painting a still-life or landscape as he felt it.

It had been almost two years since he began working at Disney Studio, in that time he had not picked up a paint brush, nor sketched for the joy of it.

He resigned.

California was no longer the haven he once thought it to be. Chicago was looking real good about now. He bought a one-way plane ticket and headed home.

May 20, 2007

Jefwin Apartments

Chicago, Chicago that wonderful town…

He thought.

He had hoped going back home was the answer to all his California miseries, but it turned out that he, himself was the problem, and he brought himself with him when he came home.

A former colleague of his at Disney had grown up in Chicago, and his parents still lived there. Upon hearing that Gill was planning on returning to Chicago, he informed Gill that his parents rented out rooms. He gave Stewart his parents address and phone number, and stated he would call them in advance of Gill.

Addressing his situation realistically, a sleeping room in a facility mostly rented to students studying at the University of Illinois, or I.I.T. was probably a good place to begin a new life, thought Stewart. After all, there was no place to go but up.

Being a mere ten minutes from Navy Pier, and no more than a fifteen minute commute on the "el" (elevated railway) to the heart of the "Loop" sounded to him like a perfect opportunity since he had no car, owned few possessions and was low on cash.

That evening he called his colleague's parents, explained who he was, his situation, and upon hearing they did have a room available, rented it sight-unseen, promising to send the first month's rent and deposit the next morning, and since he was a friend of their son, they readily agreed.

"Where did the time go?"

His cigarette, now more ash and embers than cigarette, burned his fingers.

"Damn that hurt!" Rationalizing that first cigarette didn't really count, because in reminiscing his past, his focus had been lost, and the joy of inhaling smoke into his lungs was missed.

He admitted to himself that he was a nicotine addict…but he believed two cigarettes a day would not kill him… so not having fully enjoyed smoking the first cigarette, he lit a second.

From experience he knew he would not be able to short circuit his mind from returning to his past, so to prepare himself for the journey ahead he fortified himself with two more fingers of scotch, something he did not do often, but on occasions found it helpful.

Now prepared, he again began ruminating about his past..

༆

The trip home to Chicago was relatively uneventful, save for one experience. Unable to concentrate on reading, he withdrew his sketch pad from his carry-on, and began doodling. Without any conscious thought his hand began reviewing his life in California.

First Mickey Mouse appeared on the page, followed by Donald Duck, Goofy, then other Disney characters he had drawn thousands of times. Then as if that chapter of his life had ended, his images morphed into human figures. Nudes, male, female, figures in action, figures in repose; then into portraits of people he didn't know. Face after face; profiles, full-faces, three-quarter views, faces looking up, faces looking down. Within moments he sensed the gentleman seated next to him was more interested in the drawings he was watching being created, than the book he had been reading.

Stewart looked up from his pad, and turned to his one person audience, "Hi, I draw to pass time. I draw when I think. I just draw a lot. Been doing it all my life".

"I must say you are quite talented. Within minutes I have seen you create a portfolio of images as good or better than any illustrator I have worked with. Please allow me to introduce myself. My name is Larry Cromwell. I am an art director at *Newhart and Satchie*. I too used to draw early on in my career, but now I let others do it for me. Nevertheless, I would give my eye teeth to be as talented as you. Not that I'm complaining, I love what I do. It is only when I see drawing such as yours, that I become nostalgic about my old days in art school."

"Thank you. You are very kind. My name is Stewart Gill. I am pleased to meet you. You know, I honestly can't recall a day in my life when I didn't draw. I went from the *School for the Arts* right here in Chicago, to *U.C.L.A.* for my *Bachelor of Fine Arts* degree… to my *Master's of Fine Arts* degree… to teaching drawing and painting… to Disney… to a disastrous marriage. Now having completed what I call "The California-Full-Circle, I find myself coming back to where it all began.

What I find fascinating is I don't have a clue to what's going to happen next."

Larry Cromwell couldn't help smiling at his new acquaintance's candor, while thinking to himself that fate sure works in strange ways.

"This could be a serendipitous moment. We, my company, *Newhart and Satchie,* is looking to hire someone. One of our Art Directors was recently lured away from us by BBD&O in New York City, and we need to hire someone fast. Tell you what. Here's my card. Give me a call when you are settled. I'll see what I can do for you."

They talked for most of the remaining flight into Chicago. Gill agreed to meet Larry Cromwell the following day in his office with portfolio. They would become fast friends for many years to come.

He decided to take the bus into town from the airport as a way of delaying the inevitability, at least in his own mind, of his less than triumphant return home, and as a way of helping him reacquaint himself with his former home town. Within an hour and a half, he arrived at his new abode… a rented room.

After unpacking the meager possessions he had brought to his new home, he shoved the one suitcase, and one overnight bag under the bed. Everything he owned fit into the small dresser he had in his room The good news he said to himself was he had plenty of room for new acquisitions. He sat on the corner of his bed, exhausted and mused.

"How is it possible for me to come home with the same amount, if not less luggage then I had when I first went out to California?"

With an appointment set for the following day, he decided he needed to stretch his legs badly. It had been a long, long flight from California. Since he was not far from downtown, he decided that would be his destination. This would also enable him to also locate the building where he would be interviewed the following day. He enjoyed walking in a real city. It was not Chicago he had run from, it had been his parents and the lousy weather.

During his stroll downtown, he discovered a wonderful Mexican restaurant, *Mi Casa, Su Casa*. Having acquired a taste for Mexican food during his years in California, and not having eaten all day his decision to eat here was a no-brainer.

Entering the restaurant, he was pleasantly surprised. The environment was beautifully designed and tastefully executed. There were none of the usual poorly painted murals, gaudy colors and ugly printing associated with so many Mexican restaurants. No, *Mi Casa, Su Casa* was tastefully appointed with silk-copies of indigenous Mexican foliage placed in such away that it made the diner think he/she was dining in an outdoor garden; each table sported a white table cloth, a vase with fresh flowers, and four light-blue crystal goblets turned up-side down just waiting to be turned, filled and enjoyed. The tile floor was in two shades of blue, the perfect compliment to the design of the restaurant.

Two walls sported very good reproductions: one by Diego Rivera, *The Bourgeois Family (Wall Street Banquet) and the Night of the Rich*: this was juxtaposed on the facing wall, by Thomas Hart Benton's *Arts of the West*. He was amazed at the quality of the reproductions, and more so by their choice. Both artists rallied against the evils of big cities, and both tried to monumentalize the common man. He had never really thought of the similarities imbued in these highly nationalistic men before now.

He ordered as an appetizer cheviche and as a main course, mole poblano de guajolote (turkey). And the perfect compliment to the feast, *Corona*, a great Mexican beer. The *Corona* was cold, and the food outstanding. He thought this would be a wonderful place for him and his family to share their first meal together in years.

Alas, he had never considered the possibility that his family would not feel the same.

They were to meet him at the restaurant Thursday evening 6:30 pm. Since the reunion was arranged on the TTY, and he clearly typed in a description of the restaurant, and where it was, it didn't occur to him there could be a problem. Besides, knowing they were not comfortable traveling to the city, he had told them to take a cab and he would reimburse them.

By 6:45 he was starting to worry. His parents were always prompt, and without a TTY, there was no way he could contact them. To calm his nerves down he ordered a second beer.

Stewart hadn't seen his parents and sister in years. He loved them dearly, they just had different lives. Growing up he had always felt somewhat sorry for himself. Having to act as an interface for his parents, interpret for his parents, making excuses when they did not show up for conferences and other school related activities. Now that he was older and more objective, with time on his hands, he was beginning to realize how difficult it was for them, not only being deaf in a hearing world, but trying to rear a hearing child.

Being hearing, he had a choice; they on the other hand, were at the mercy of others. They had to always try to have others understand, and always having to live with the intolerance around them. They were the ones who really had it rough, not him His sister, knowing that if she was lucky would have the life of her parents, dreaming of wanting more, but with the knowledge it would never happen. He had choices, she didn't. He could pick up and go anywhere at any time, she could not. He was sure she pondered the question, why, why was she born deaf, and her brother not? Same parents. Why her?

Checking his watch again, and looking around the restaurant and it's environs, he noticed his family standing outside the restaurant busily signing to each other, making no effort to enter the premises. Stewart signaled to the waiter that he would be right back.

With relief and a big, genuine smile on his face, truly excited, he walked outside the restaurant to greet his family. What he encountered was his father furiously signing, "no, no go there! No, no will not go in! Mistake. I told you mistake!" His mother had tears rolling down her cheeks, and his sister was looking at her brother with scorn.

How could he have been that stupid! His parents had never been to a fancy restaurant in downtown Chicago, for that matter a fancy restaurant anywhere. They could not bear people staring at them, as hearing people so often look at deaf people signing to each other. They were frightened, they were embarrassed. He had been an insensitive ass.

His family was lost in a hearing world. His parents had not used their voices in years, had poor lip reading skills, and were not comfortable writing. His sister, though possessing some oral skills, would not dare risk using her voice in an environment composed of only hearing people. And barely being proficient in English, seeing words in Spanish frightened the hell out of her.

Stewart walked up to his parents and sister, gave them a big hug and many kisses, signed to them to wait there one minute. He had to settle his bill. Then they would take a cab to the deaf club in the old neighborhood.

Though the big homecoming meal he had planned turned out to be fast-frozen sandwiches, nuked, and served on paper plates, and the margarita's, bottles of beer, not even Corona, the reunion was successful, and they were all just glad to be a family again.

Welcome home Stewart Gill.

The next day, armed with his portfolio he went to see Larry Cromwell at *Newhart and Satchie.*

The old expression, "timing is everything" was never more true.

The company was not only in need of an art director, but was also looking to hire a studio illustrator. The previous studio illustrator who had occupied the job for the past twelve years suddenly had a heart attack, and would not be returning. The president and creative director agreed with Larry Cromwell that a man with the skills of Stewart Gill could easily take the place of not only the illustrator, but quite possibly handle both jobs.

The position of art director/illustrator was offered to Stewart that very morning at a salary slightly less than he was making at Disney. Though expecting more, Gill rationalized, "bird in hand, was worth more than two in bush." To be gainfully employed, earning a decent salary in less than one week of returning home can't be sneezed at.

To sweeten the pot, not wanting to lose this seemingly "God-sent" illustrator, yet not wanting to pay any more than was necessary, *Newhart and Satchie* informed Gil that it was a long-standing company policy to pay new-hires slightly under standard for the first six months. Then, after the semi-annual review, they almost guaranteed a hefty pay raise would be forthcoming.

Very quickly Stewart proved his worth. Be it packaging, point-of-sale, point-of-purchase, presentations, or advertisements, he could satisfy the client's need in any style they, and the art director he was supporting decided. With his skills all he needed was a sample of the style desired and he could render it with ease; not plagiarize, but capture the essence of the desired style.

Not only was his ability to create imagery superior, but his design skills were not far behind. Added to the myriad of skills he possessed was an inexhaustible energy. He never turned down an assignment. No matter how much work they threw at him, he never complained, and always met every deadline.

Each assignment was a challenge, and Stewart loved challenges.

Within the first month of his employ many of the account executives started coming to him directly by-passing other art directors. His now colleague, Larry Cromwell tried talking some sense into him. "Stewart, you have nothing to prove, everyone knows you are talented, slow down. Tell the account executives to follow office procedure and stay with the art directors assigned to the account. You are really starting to piss off a number of people. Slow down, be part of the team"

Stewart thanked his friend, and said he would take his words under advisement.

He didn't.

Within three months he was being assigned as much art direction work as illustration. His bosses were happy, the account executives were happy, many of his colleagues were not.

Nevertheless, Stewart was pleased with himself. Being a work-a-holic, being busy was something that fed his soul. He had almost no social life, and had not made many friends. Working weekends, and evenings made no difference to him. He was doing what he loved to do. In fact when he wasn't busy doing work for *Newhart and Satchie*, he was free-lancing, taking in work of all kinds. He created Information Graphics (illustrative charts and graphs) for the *Research Bureau of America*, designed and rendered dozens of maps for *Hammond Maps*, and art directed and illustrated a number of lines of packaging for *Bristol Meyers*.

Six months went by, seven, eight months with no review. After reminding his bosses of the terms of employment they had agreed upon... still nothing happened. All he got from his bosses were lame excuses which were becoming less believable with each passing day.

In conversations he had during lunches with Larry Cromwell, he was told, warned that he had caused a lot of distress in the agency. Good, reliable, talented veterans were threatening to quit if he wasn't towed in. His bosses felt they were between a rock and a hard place; not wanting to lose him, but also not wanting to lose veteran staff people. Their strategy was do nothing, and hope the problem would resolve itself. Face-to-face they told Gill how much they valued him; what a great job he was doing; everyone thought the world of him, but to please understand that things had slowed down, profits were down, to please have patience.

Yataty-yataty-yaytaty.

Stewart had run out of patience. On Friday, eleven am, after getting his weekly pay check, eight months and two weeks after being hired, he walked into his bosses' office and told them to go fuck themselves. He quit!

With that he walked out of *Newhart and Satchie* into the sunshine and smiled.

"No one treats me like shit!"

Talent cannot be denied.

Over the course of the next six years Stewart managed a multi-image/multi-media company, was part owner of two design studios and one advertising agency. He also managed to get married and divorced twice, paying out almost as much in alimony as he was earning.

He was stacking up some impressive numbers for a little kid from Chicago with deaf parents.

The kinks in his armor, his Achilles heel, seemed to be his need to continually prove himself, and a well-honed ability to trust the wrong people and alienate the right people. His work ethic, and love of imagery had transformed themselves into an aggressiveness, and at times an acrid personality.

He prided himself in his fairness and honesty. He was brutally forthright, and could not understand why others could not be like himself.

The only friend he managed to keep was Larry Cromwell. They always found a way to have lunch once to twice-a-week. It was during the last lunch, that his friend told Stewart that his sister was flying in from New York City later that week, and was going to stay with him and his wife for the week. She was thirty-two years old, single, attractive, and bright, actually brilliant!. He thought Stewart and his sister would hit it off. Would he like to join the Cromwell's for dinner Friday night?

Stewart, not having been on a date, nor for that matter, with any woman not connected to business, in the last few months readily agreed.

They did better than hit it off. It was like sparks arcing two live wires. Both A-personalities, both absolutely-sure of themselves, and both very, very aggressive.

Samantha Lewis-Cromwell though born in Chicago was for all practical purposes a tried-and-true New Yorker. From the age of seventeen when she went off to attend college at Columbia University, she stated to the world that her home was, and would always be New York City. She was true to her word. She stayed on at Columbia to earn a Master's degree in English Literature; worked at a number of advertising agency's copy departments, then moved on to the *Village Voice*. Within five years she moved up from their copy department to assistant copy editor, to senior news editor.

She was good at what she did, and as tough as anyone around her. She loved the newspaper business, loved the *Village Voice* and loved Greenwich Village. She loved the Village so much that when a warehouse building being converted to loft apartments, a block from Bleaker Street in the heart of the Village came available, she went into hock, and borrowed a large sum of money from her brother to buy it. She then rehabbed the loft into an elegant two-bedroom, 3,200 square feet domicile she called home.

From an innocent family dinner at the Cromwell's... to a torrid week of touring, dining and love making, Stewart and Samantha were not apart for more than a moment or two.

Once introductions and pleasant, but meaningless small talk was accomplished over cocktails and appetizers, Samantha, having heard about Stewart from her brother, wasted no time engaging him into what at first was a conversation, which then blossomed into a discussion, and ripened into a week-long dialogue on what the writer Henry James once proposed. He stated there were three questions which could be, and in his opinion should be, asked of an artist's work.

What was the artist trying to achieve? Did she/he succeed? And was the effort worth doing?

Those three questions were still being heatedly discussed when he dropped her off at the airport five days later.

He could not get over her ardor for life, and her frenetic, insatiable thirst for discovery and experience. What he didn't expect, and what surprised him even more, was her knowledge of Art, and her ability to make it come alive. For the first time in his life he was hearing his passion for painting and drawing being described by her words.

It was amazing!

Finally, after more than two days and nights of answering her questions and reacting to her, it was his turn.

"Where are *you* going Samantha? What makes *you* laugh? What makes *you* cry? Is there any one-thing *you* want to accomplish more than anything else in your life."

It was during these discussions that she spoke to him of a book she wanted to write. She even had a working title for it: *The Blessing and the Curse.* The theme being how, in her opinion the gift the artist is given is clearly a double edged sword. The gift of being able to create, and the curse of never being satisfied with the work created. Her book was the story of his life. She understood that once the artist's passion which emanates from his/her soul gives birth to an idea, it can only be turned into a work of art by being tightly crafted by discipline, technique and an unfailing determination.

They were cut from the same bolt of material. The only difference between them was that she used words and phrases, and he used paints and brushes.

Since he was between assignments, going nowhere in particular he was very receptive, when she suggested he try his luck in New York. She believed she could find him work at the paper, and he could stay with her as long as he liked.

He readily agreed.

Sadly it only took four months for the chemistry which brought them together, to begin to drive them apart. Passion, idealism, righteousness, and boundless energy without the balance of patience, gentility, flexibility and rest, created an atmosphere so charged, sparks began to fly, and patience eroded.

For some reason Stewart was never able to ascertain, good fortune always seemed to step into his life at a time of need. From Dr. Rosen, to Coach Peters, to Dr. Engers, to Larry Cromwell, to Samantha Lewis-Cromwell, to his college roommate, Tom Popko, who became a matrimonial lawyer living in Chicago, who saved his ass with his divorces. Something, someone seemed to be there for him.

Now once again good fortune found its way to him.

It was during his third month working at the *Village Voice*, where he was producing a weekly political comic strip, and a variety of illustrations on an as-need basis, that representatives of the newly organized *International Facility for Students who are*

Deaf (I.F.S.D.) came visiting the paper seeking out publicity for their new program. This new program was housed at Brookside University in upstate New York.

The managing editor, after hearing the goals, aspirations and scope of the program, and not wanting to undertake any additional work for himself, escorted the three gentlemen to Samantha Lewis-Cromwell's office. On the way, he explaining that she was the *Village Voice's* chief copy editor, one of the most talented, dynamic reporters he had on staff, and assured them that Samantha would do her best to help them garner publicity for this new program.

Being a very bright woman, Samantha having sensed her days and nights with Stewart Gill were numbered, and upon hearing of the creation of *I.F.S.D.* knew immediately here was a solution that would serve all parties involved, extremely well.

She loved Stewart, more than she imagined she could love a man, but knew after three months she could not live with him for much longer. She respected him for his ethics and morality, but his brashness and twenty-four hour a day intensity was not only self-destructive, but totally exhausting to her at the same time.

For Stewart, after three months of producing less work then he had produced in three weeks in the past, he was becoming frustrated. The paper was more than satisfied with the work he was doing, but basically, he was simply bored. Not being challenged, not having an outlet for his energy he was becoming antsy and was leading towards testiness. Not one in great control of his feelings, it was beginning to take it's toll on their relationship.

Knowing his family was deaf, that he was fluent in sign language, and that his fondest memories were of his days teaching at *U.C.L.A.*, Samantha quickly arranged for Stewart to meet the gentlemen from *I.F.D.S.* Within minutes, the four people she had brought together were, speaking, signing, laughing and in general impressing each other.

A more perfect match could not be formed.

Within one month after the initial meeting, the university made Stewart Gill an offer to join it's faculty at the rank of Assistant Professor. He would be working with students who were deaf, who were studying for their degree in the *College of the Arts, Crafts and Imaging Sciences.*

He was assured *Brookside* would be a perfect place for a person with his energy and capacity to tackle myriads of projects simultaneously.

The salary they offered was to his mind embarrassingly low, yet he understood money did not bring happiness, at least not in his life, and the opportunity to really do something that had meaning, something for others, was just too good to pass up.

On their last night together, Samantha wanted it to be spectacular. After all, what they had shared, even if it was for a short time, most people didn't experience in a lifetime.

Other than the written word, and visual imagery, discourse on all aspects of life, love-making and food were their three passions.

Discourse, in their time together, began with "good morning," and ended with "good night."

Love-making, was a result of an animal magnetism which drew them together, and kept them there until they literally passed out.

Food, whether shopping, preparing or eating was something they both loved, and although their preferences were different, hers Italian, and his Mexican, each loved to share each other's passion. That was why she decided their last meal would be one she would make, and her farewell gourmet gift to him.

In the business of art and news, *deadline* was king. And since today was to be his last day in New York City, he felt he had to finish his last strip for the *Village Voice,* thus fulfilling his responsibility by meeting the deadline and being able to walk away from the job with his head held high.

That last morning he left for work at seven forty-five in the morning for a brisk walk to work. On his way out he waved a kiss to Samantha. Twice after actually kissing her in the morning, they ended up spending the rest of the morning in bed. He would not allow it to happen a third time.

In a way Samantha was relieved yet sad, knowing the end of this unbelievable relationship was near. Then again, when creating gourmet masterpieces she preferred being alone. To her preparing Italian food was not only a multi-sensorial experience, but one in which she could lose herself in fantasy without being self-conscious.

She had evolved a routine she never varied from. First she put on her favorite recording, *Madam Butterfly* featuring Renata Tribaldi as soprano. Then she poured herself a glass of *Pinot Grigio* (a crisp white wine which was flavorful and soothing) into her favorite wine glass (it didn't matter what time she was cooking, be it eight am, or eight pm… wine was part of the experience). Step three was donning her favorite apron bearing the words, "*ars longa, vita brevis*" (Art is long, life is short).

Now with the preliminaries completed, she was ready to get serious.

Before leaving for work that morning, Samantha asked Stewart to stop at the liquor store on his way home and pick up a bottle of *Lagrein Rosato*, a pink wine from a northern province, which in her opinion was the only pink wine she had ever tasted with real character, and a bottle of *Venegazzu*, a hearty red with equally robust character.

Since Samantha loved and lived the good life, and wine was a major element of the good life, she would not settle for anything she believed was not the best. Being a very good customer, the local liquor store was more than happy to special order specific Italian wines for her.

At the precise moment Stewart exited the apartment, Samantha got down to work. She had spent a lot of time planning the entire evening, and what she planned, she would accomplish.

To begin the evenings festivities the cocktails, always served from her bar in her living room, were to be *Crown Royal Manhattans* with a twist of lemon peel. She had put in a lot of effort convincing Stewart that a *Crown Royal Manhattan* was a far superior drink than a mere *Margarita*, and for the sake of unity and love-making, he had let her believe she had taught him something. Besides, if he couldn't get a *Margarita, Crown Royal* was a pretty good second choice.

The appetizer she picked to usher in the cocktails was *Uova Sode Agli Spinaci* (hard boiled eggs stuffed with a puree of spinach, parmesan and cream cheese, topped with salt, pepper and a dash of nutmeg. Since it is almost impossible to cook for two people she made two dozen.

"A good nosh at a later time."

The first course to accompany the *Lagrein Rosato,* the pink wine Stewart had purchased earlier in the day was to be a *Insalata di Fungi e Frutti di Mare* (a salad of raw mushrooms and cooked shellfish, prawns and octopus). To appreciate it's delicacy and flavors, it had to be served at room temperature with extra virgin olive oil and garnished sparingly with parsley.

The soup portion of the meal would be a *Zuppa di Castagne* (chestnut soup). The savory flavor of the soup when served with slices of fried bread literally enhanced the taste-buds and prepared them for the main course.

For the main course, the *coup de grace,* Samantha planned a *Casoeula* (Milanese stewed pork). It was probably her favorite Italian dish. It was made with a lean pork roast, Italian pork sausage, bacon rind, carrots, onion, celery, white wine, flour, butter, salt, pepper and a bay leaf. It was served with white cabbage, quartered, which is prepared separately and added to Casoeula a half hour before serving. Thus blending the flavors, according to Samantha in a magical manner. The white hand-made porcelain serving platter made in *Tuscany,* was large enough to display the prepared fried polenta rounds at the outer rim with the Casoeula in the middle crowned by the quartered cabbage.

Samantha though a more colorful, savory dish was not possible.

Since all fine dining had to end with a sweet, Samantha planned a Zabaione (a custard prepared with Marsala wine, served warm in heated glasses).

A memorable dinner? Oh yes, it would be the most memorable diner of his life

All could not have been better. Stewart came home with the wine feeling very good about himself. He had completed all his work at the paper, and was told he did a great job, and they hated to lose him, but understood. If he ever needed a glowing reference, he should not hesitate to contact them.

He couldn't remember another time in his life when a parting of a job, company or person(s) made him feel good.

Samantha, as Samantha always did, had planned and timed everything to perfection.

As he walked into the living room she was seductively seated at the bar. To her left on the bar, were two elegant pieces of stemware chilling in a bucket of ice. Next to the ice, a pitcher of Manhattans, a bottle of maraschino cherries, and a jar of *Angostura* bitters there if he wanted to modify the taste slightly. Being who he was, she knew he would have to alter in in some minute way, which would then make him feel in control.

Completing the scene was a depression-glass platter beautifully displaying the *Uova Sode Agli Spinaci,* the deviled-eggs

Yet that all paled next to her. She was pure elegance. She was wearing a v-neck, ecru-colored, silk caftan showing a perfect amount of cleavage, with a white shawl loosely wrapped around her shoulders. The silver earrings and necklace of Afghani design, though large in size, were on this occasion the perfect fit.

She looked like a Goddess.

Not expecting to see her this way, he suddenly stopped in his tracks wondering if maybe their parting tomorrow could be a mistake.

It wasn't. Deep inside he knew it. Yes, she was the most unique woman he had ever met. But he also knew that if he stayed any longer this wonderful chapter of his life would turn ugly.

The dinner was scrumptious; their love-making electric and their good-byes filled with hope and happiness.

As a parting gift, he unwrapped a portrait he had painted of her, and she gave him an eleven by fourteen silver framed quote by T.S.Eliot.

"The more perfect the artist, the more completely separate in him will be the man who suffers and the mind which creates..."

By ten am the next morning Stewart was hugging Samantha for the last time. Not a word was uttered. Exiting the apartment, with a bag in each hand, not looking back, he descended the steps, experienced the cool fresh air, and hailed a cab.

"LaGuardia Airport please, American Airlines terminal."

He never looked back.

May 20, 2007

Jefwin Apartments

Back to the present.

It was hard for him to believe how abstract time could be. Shaking his head, he repeated the question he had asked himself a moment ago...

"Where did the years go ?"

"Ah, the frivolity, and rashness of youth wasted on the young."

Seeing his image in the mirror on the other side of the room brought a smile to his face. Shaking his head, and taking the last sip of scotch in his glass, he bellowed out, "Cut the shit Gill!

It has been a great journey. He didn't regret anything. It might not have worked out as he originally planned, but regrets? No way"

Lighting up his third cigarette that day, he returned to his past, and thought about how and why possessions had been important to him.

Growing up he didn't have much, and hadn't needed much. As he got older, and his world began to expand, *things* began to represent success. Acquiring *things* felt good, and it was important to him to feel good.

At that moment he became aware someone was knocking at the door. He arose from his chair, proceeded to the front door, and opened it.

"Mr. Gill your limousine is here to take you to campus."

"Sorry I didn't hear you knocking."

That's okay, the maintenance man said, I only knocked a couple of times. The driver of the limousine, asked me to tell you he will wait for you at the front gate."

"Thank you, tell him I will be right there."

Tidying up his mess, he picked up his glass, put it into the sink, fetched his wallet, looked at himself in the mirror, and said to himself, "I can't say I am living the life or *Riley*, but I have to admit, at this moment, I feel pretty damn good, and I don't look half bad either."

Before leaving, and for no particular reason looked all around at his apartment.

He would never see it again

Since Stewart Gill lived closest to the university he was scheduled to be the last passenger to be picked up. Entering the limo, he was greeted by his three colleagues who cried out in unison, "What took you so long?"

"You must know to look this good takes time."

His colleagues, in deference to this man's reputation, speaking and using the one sign they all knew bellowed out, "Bullshit!"

The limousine was equipped with seats on both sides to enable passengers to face one another. In the middle was a table designed to hold four bottles of liquor, eight glasses and a bucket of ice. As Stewart was buckling his seat belt, Stan poured him a good two fingers of scotch in a glass filled with ice.

"Here you go Stewart, you have some catching up to do. We've been in this bus for the last half hour, and we just couldn't wait for you."

"Thank you. I appreciate your civility, and understand your impatience."

"And now that we are all here…"

Earl lifted the glass in his hand, an action followed by his three colleagues…

"Here's to us. May our lives continue to be filled with wondrous times, may good health be our constant companion, and may we never become so enamored with ourselves that we forget where we came from."

Stan added:

"As King Solomon once said, Our life is short and miserable, and there is no cure when man/woman comes to his/her end, and no one has been known to return from the abode of the dead.

We were born as a venture, and hereafter we shall be as we never existed, because the breath in our nostrils is smoke, and reason is a spark in the beating of our hearts; when it is quenched, the body will turn to ashes, be forgotten, and no one will remember what we have done.

So come, let us enjoy the good things that exist…Let us have our fill of costly wines and perfumes, and let us not miss the spring flowers…"

As if by plan, all eyes turned to Stewart who added:

"If a man…" turning to Nan, forgive me dear colleague, let me begin again.

"If a woman or a man does not keep pace with his/her companions, perhaps it is because she/he hears a different drummer. Let him/her step to the music which she/he hears, however measured or far away."

Nan beaming at the conviviality and collegiality of the moment spoke:

"Success is dangerous. One begins to copy oneself, and to copy one's self is more dangerous than to copy others, it leads to sterility.

So let us drink to passion, talent, intelligence and to modesty"

All four outstanding teachers downed their glasses, sat back and contemplated their future.

May 20, 2009

7:00pm

Brookside University, (the recently completed) Miller Field house.

The room was filled with 700 tables, seating 8 persons per table, was completely sold out. Added to the horde of guests was a separate area set aside to accommodate major media from across the country, and the international community. When the news was released that the Vice President of the United States was to be addressing the audience, requests for space was a constant. So vigorous were the requests for seats, that a special telecast was set up, via cable, to facilitate all parties on and off campus.

The audience was becoming restless. Dinner had been served, and eaten. Coffee was served, and now cold. The faculty honorees who were slated to each give a presentation, prior to the Vice President's remarks, were now forty minutes late.

The Vice President, the keynote speaker, the real reason this celebration had become a media event, sent word to the Provost that he was on a very tight schedule, and scheduled to leave almost immediately after the completion of his speech. He had agreed to come only as a personal favor to the university's President Ellingwood, and *Air-Force One* was waiting to take him back to Washington.

Needing no other reminders, Dr. Bullward, Provost and Chief academic officer of Brookside arose from his seat on the platform, and moved to the dais.

"Ladies and gentlemen, may I have your attention… please. I appreciate your patience and understanding. To be honest, I don't know what has delayed the limousine with our honored faculty. I am sure there is an explanation. The company providing the livery service has been contacted. It seems they have lost contact with the driver, and have sent out other vehicles, just in case there was a mishap on the road.

"The Vice President has just reminded me of the tightness of his schedule, and has requested that his address start the evening off, instead of concluding it. I agreed. So if everyone would please return to their tables, take their seats, this evenings festivities will begin."

An eerie silence slowly replaced the din of the cacophony of thousands of people sharing a limited space.

Looking around, seeing almost everyone seated, Dr. Bullward nodded to the Vice President, turned and smiled at the audience.

"Ladies and Gentlemen, this is a great day for Brookside University. Not only are we honoring outstanding teaching by four of the best faculty members…anywhere, but we have the honor and great privilege to have the Vice President of the United States with us.

"Vice President Foxworthy has served this great country in a variety of capacities for more than 30 years. Six years serving in the House of Representatives for the great state of Maryland; eighteen years as Senator of that state, four years as Secretary of Education, and the last two years filling the shoes of the late Secretary Miller as Secretary of State for the previous administration.

When now President Ownes was nominated to represent his party in the race for the presidency, he wasted no time announcing in his acceptance speech that Myron Foxworthy was to be his running mate. Saying, and I quote: "There is no man or woman whom I know who is more respected in the Congress than Dr. Foxworthy. His bipartisanship, his intelligence, his negotiating skills and his dedication to this country has gained him universal support in every position he has served, as well as the people he has worked with."

"I can go on, and on, and mention this man's meritorious accomplishments in education, in statesmanship and in the political arena, but as the Vice President has informed me, he has a plane to catch."

A quiet laughter could be heard as some of the anxiety of the audience seemed to dissipate.

As Dr. Bullward was concluding his introduction to the Vice President, a messenger burst through the doors and ran up to the head table, which also served as the speaker's platform.

With tears streaking down his face the messenger handed a message to the Provost, after which he simply collapsed on the floor in a state of shock.

After an initial gasp, not a sound could be heard. Everyone sat frozen in their chairs.

Scanning the memo, and after a number of aborted attempts to speak, the Provost found his voice.

"I have been directed to read this memo I have just been handed. It is addressed to the President of Brookside University, myself, the media, this evening's attendees, the Vice President and the President of the United States.

Anyone who knows me, or of me knows I can't abide intimidation of any sort. "

Taking a deep breath, and scanning the audience he then continued.

"I usually don't take direction very well, and a large part of me at this very moment is screaming silent expletives deleted, but duty must prevail. I believe I have no choice at this point but to follow the instructions I have been given, and read this letter.

To the people of the United States:

You have recently read in your media about a rash of killings that has occurred since March, claiming the lives of 53 people. From Samson, Alabama, to Oakland, California, to Santa Clara, California, to Carthage, North Carolina, to Binghamton, New York to Pittsburgh, Pennsylvania to Graham, Washington, and tomorrow… you will read about four more deaths that occurred one mile from Brookside University.

These were not random deaths, as your media has attempted to distort. These and others are the work of al-Qaeda, the freedom fighters. We, the sons of Allah, have taken this course of action to demonstrate the righteousness of our cause and to show you that you are powerless to stop us. You are vulnerable not only in Iraq, Pakistan, Afghanistan, Lebanon and all over the Near East, but right here on the shores of your own country.

The devastation of the Twin Towers in New York City should be a reminder of our capabilities. We will continue to reign terror upon you until you cease to reign terror upon us. We are not suicide bombers, we are messengers of Allah. Our message is clear, get out of our lands. We did not invade you. You invaded us. Your president, using lies as justification and unprovoked by us, initiated a reign of terror that began in Iraq and has now spread across the Near East, causing the death of hundreds of thousands of innocent civilians.

In Iraq alone, more than 110,000 Iraqis have died in violence since the 2003 U.S.-led invasion. You mourn over the deaths of thousands, we mourn over the deaths of hundreds of thousands. You call us liars and devils, but who lied to his own people and the world about not sanctioning torture? Then, when exposed as a liar, went on to justify it on the basis of it's results.

Your government orchestrated a walk-out by some 40 diplomats from Britain, France and other European countries at the United Nations Conference on racism, when Iranian President Mahmoud Ahmadinejad accused the West of using the Holocaust as a pretext for aggression against Palestinians. Yet you fund and arm Israel as it denies the Palestinians it's rightful homelands.

You, who have a history of interfering in the internal affairs of legally, duly elected governments from Paraguay to Panama, from Iraq to Iran, from the Bay of Pigs in Cuba to Columbia, from Haiti to Afghanistan, you accuse us of promoting violence and chaos, when you are actually the nation of evil.

Your own Frederick Douglas has said: "Those who profess to favor freedom, and yet deprecate agitation, are men who want crops without plowing up the ground."

We seek freedom to pursue our way of life. We seek it in our lands, not yours. Therefore the four educators who lost their lives tonight when we blew up the vehicle they were riding in were not our enemies. They were merely pawns in our battle to regain our lands and practice our way of life. They were our form of agitation. Once the media reported the Vice President would be in attendance at the ceremony to honor the four faculty persons, we knew that this would be for us a "perfect storm," planned and carried out our mission successfully. Praise be to Allah!

We knew the deaths of Stanley MacKeon, Earl Starkvisor, Nan Alderage and Stewart Gill would afford us the opportunity of promoting our cause, and gain us national and international attention. Their destruction would indicate the weakness of a once great nation in the eyes of the world, and act to convince others not to get involved aiding and abetting our enemy. By this act we have shown that the United States' inability to protect it's own clearly proves the internal deterioration occurring in this land.

The elimination of those four great teachers in one thundering explosion, scattering thousands of pieces of metal as well as hundreds of pieces of human flesh for more than a mile, should, and to our way of thinking, will bring terror into the hearts and the minds of your citizens. It is our fervent hope that our act encourages your citizens to bring pressure upon their government to change its course of action. And finally, be assured that anyone who helps promote your evil, can and will be made targets.

"Our message is strong, our determination inexhaustible, and our mission true. Allah will be served. You have seventy-two hours to announce the beginning of troop withdrawals across the entire middle-east. If no announcement is made, attacks such as the one this evening will begin again, and will occur with greater frequency across the face of your nation.

Riad Hassan al-Baghdadi

Sons of Allah"

As Provost Bullward ended his reading of al-Baghdadi's letter the silence in the room became deafening. No one moved. It seemed no one even took a breath.

Within moments, which could have passed for hours, Vice President Foxworthy arose from his seat, approached Dr. Bullard and asked him for permission to speak. The Provost almost mechanically nodded his head and backed away from the podium. With a sternness and a determination only seen on the faces of men and women clear as to their task, he began.

"Ladies and Gentlemen:

The good Lord raised up this mighty nation to be a home of the brave who will flourish in a free land. As God is my witness, I swear to fight the demonic evil that has threatened our way of life with acts of terror and lies, that they hope justify their fanaticism.

I have been given permission to speak for the President of the United States at times of crisis or when he is otherwise occupied. I'm quite sure the President will address the nation later. For now I speak for myself, the President, and for every citizen of the world who values freedom, humanity and integrity.

The insanity, the carnage, the evil we have heard about tonight is despicable and inhumane by any standard, and/or any religious belief. I give you my word the scum who committed these unthinkable acts of violence will be hunted down and brought to justice.

Freedom has a price, a very high price. At times it not only demands the lives of our finest men and women on the battlefield, but is sometimes sadly paid for with the lives of our brightest and most talented at home. In this day and age, peace can only be kept if we remain vigilant and strong. We will not allow peace or freedom to be torn from our grasp because of our lack of strength or will. Those who want to bury us, to do away with freedom of choice, of religion, of speech will in the end be interned in hell for eternity.

To a larger extent these acts of terrorism and the carnage it brings, shows all of us in the United States the importance of the struggle for peace and security around the world. Aggression by terror is an act of cowardice. The fanatics who perpetrate these violent acts do so not to promote religious fervor, but do so to gain power. Power over the peaceful, power over the needy, power to deny others the right to be or not to be.

We as a nation have been, and will continually pledge to extend ourselves to help, teach and cultivate freedom, so that all nations of the world have the opportunity to reap the gifts of freedom and democracy.

On October 26, 1963, President John F. Kennedy was at Amherst College to participate in a ceremony to honor the poet Robert Frost. Now, as I look around at the faces of members of this audience, I feel it is appropriate for me today to freely quote and paraphrase a portion of that speech. He said:

"I look forward to a great future for America, a future in which our country will match its military strength with our moral restraint, it's wealth with our wisdom, its power with our purpose. I look forward to an America which will not be afraid of grace and beauty, which will protect the beauty of our natural environment, which will preserve the great of American houses and squares and parks of our national past, and which will build handsome and balanced cities for our future.

I look forward to an America which will reward achievement in the arts and sciences as we reward achievement in business or statecraft. I look forward to an America which will steadily raise the standards of artistic, scientific and humanistic accomplishments and which will steadily enlarge cultural, and educational opportunities for all of our citizens. And I look forward to an America which commands respect throughout the world not only for its strength but for its civilization as well. And I look forward to a world which will be safe not only for democracy and diversity but for personal distinction."

Robert Frost was often skeptical about projects for human improvement, yet I do not think he would disdain this hope. As he wrote during the uncertain days of the Second War:

"Take human nature altogether since time began...

And it must be a little more in favor of man,

Say a fraction of one percent of the very least...

Our hold on this planet wouldn't have so increased."

"Because of Mr. Frost's life and work, because of the life and work of this college, and because of the life and work of your outstanding professors our hold on this planet has been increased.

As I said earlier, we will not rest until each and every person responsible for these heinous crimes have been brought to justice.

God bless the families and friends of Stanley MacKeon, Earl Starkvisor, Nan Alderage-Gates and Stewart Gill, God bless all assembled here this evening, and God bless America."

EPILOGUE

To My Readers:

I have written this novel to pay homage to the human condition, and its capacity to adapt, excel and overcome adversity. I understand and respect that some believe everything that occurs is pre-determined. I however fervently believe that the circuitous journey we call "living" is a matter of happenstance. It is our capacity to adjust, some call our genius, that enables us and insures our continuance.

The book *"Dewey On Education"* concludes with, "For the creation of a democratic society we need an educational system where the process of moral-intellectual development is in practice as well as in theory, a cooperative transaction of inquiry engaged in by free, independent human beings who treat ideas and the heritage of the past as means and methods for the future enrichment of life quantitatively and qualitatively, who use the good attained for the discovery and establishment of something better."

Jack Slutzky